M000202774

BRUTAL SIN

EDEN SUMMERS

DEDICATION

For those who like damaged goods. I hope you enjoy Brute.

CHAPTER ONE

*P*amela slid her bare thighs onto the bar stool, feigning relaxation even though the sensation was illusive.

Whimpers and groans filled her ears, along with the rhythmic slap of naked, sweaty bodies. At one time, she'd thrived on this atmosphere. The lascivious environment had invigorated her. Awakened her.

Until the excitement wore off and desperation set in.

Escaping to the Vault of Sin had been her monthly ritual for almost two years. She'd started out optimistic, hoping to replace the void her husband's death had gouged into her chest with the delicious thrill of the exclusive sex club. Now, the bright hope had faded to black, making her bitter and resentful. There was nobody here for her. No one to give her what she needed. What she craved.

"Are you looking for company, sweetie?"

From the corner of her eye, she took in the man beside her. With the gentle tone of one word—*sweetie*—she could tell his aim for the night was to role play in genres unsuitable to her palate. She didn't want to be his good little girl. She

1

didn't require a pedestal or the touch of a delicate hand. Her desires were far more complex than that.

"I'm good, thanks."

It was time to face the harsh reality. Her sex life would forever be on a downward slide. Her marriage to a man who had pinpoint precision on her libido had ruined her for future lovers. She needed to stop wasting time on men who lacked the skill and patience to get her off. She'd squandered enough Saturday nights already, spent months upon months playing with men who refused to take non-verbal cues.

"You sure?" He placed his hand against the ribbons tying the back of her corset, now entranced with the navy-blue flecks in the material sparkling in the bar light. The boned lingerie, along with the silken panties she currently wore, were a present from her late husband, Lucas. One of the last presents he'd given her. "You look lonely."

She sighed. Yep, she definitely needed to move on. Now men weren't even taking verbal cues. "Not lonely. Just alone. There's a difference." She swiveled on the stool and slid to her feet. "And besides, we've been together before. It isn't something I want to repeat."

"Aww, honey, from memory, we had a lot of fun."

"*You* had a lot of fun." She bit her tongue to stop elaborating.

His brows pulled tight, encouraging her to walk away in case he interjected with an insult of his own. When she'd first arrived at the Vault, the other patrons had considered her shy and apprehensive. They hadn't seen past her exterior. They hadn't attempted to look deeper.

To them, she resembled a shallow, neglected puddle, when the reality was an expanse of tumultuous ocean. She knew exactly what she was searching for. The checklist was small but specific. And apparently, each item was more rare than a unicorn.

2

Her feet stopped of their own accord as she came to the open doorway of one of the side rooms. Zoe, another regular club patron, was on the sofa along the wall, her two men paying homage to her scantily-clad body with such sweet finesse it made Pamela's eyes burn.

The threat of tears wasn't due to weakness or heartbreak. These were tears of frustration. Of utter annoyance and anger. Why was it so difficult to find a man in tune with her needs, the way these men were in tune with Zoe's?

Everywhere she turned, sexual chemistry stared back at her. The bartender, Shay, had it with her manager boyfriend, Leo. Then there was T.J. and his wife, Cassie, along with every other duo inside the secretive walls of the carnal club.

Maybe her appetite was the problem.

Her desires were too specific. She had no use for sweet affection. She craved finesse in a more dominant form. The skill of a man who could inspire an orgasm mentally as well as physically. *Damn it*. Was she being overly critical? It wasn't as if she expected a stranger to learn everything about her in one touch. Problem was, some men still had no clue after three orgasms.

Theirs.

Not hers.

"They're good together, aren't they?" The smooth drawl came from a man at her back. "They adore her."

"Yes, they do." She closed her eyes briefly and forced down the instinct to fling another rejection. "But I'm looking for something a little more..."

"What?"

She shrugged. Pointing out specifics seemed equivalent to gifting a completed puzzle. Where was the fun in that?

"Whatever it is, I'm happy to help."

Her last slivers of hope faded with each breath. "I want to be controlled." The admission came with a wince. She

3

shouldn't be encouraging more opportunities for disappointment. There'd already been enough.

"Hmm." His thighs leaned into her, his unmistakable erection nestling against her ass. "I can control you, princess."

An arm wrapped around her waist. The touch light, delicate—a man playing a dominant role he had no idea how to perfect.

She turned, seeing him for the first time, his hand now draped over the low of her back. He was attractive enough. A soft hazel gaze, smooth skin, and neatly cut brown hair. What he didn't have was the *zing*. The buzz. The commanding presence in his eyes.

"Not tonight." She pulled away, only to be stopped by his tightening grip.

"You'll stay," he ordered.

A shiver ran down her spine. It could've been a delicious thrill, the start of something promising, only his features didn't match his tone. He was a scared kitten behind that hold. There was no conviction. No power.

"Take your hand off me," she grated.

It wasn't easy to play an unfamiliar role. It took balls. Large ones. And the man she needed required cojones the size of a rhino, not a mouse.

"I'm sorry." His hand fell, his balk of regret reigniting her frustration. "I was only trying to—"

"I know." She pasted on a smile, determined to fight her bitchy attitude into submission. "And I appreciate the attempt."

It wasn't his fault she was already edgy from the impending sexual sobriety. She needed to remove her toxic attitude from this place of bodily worship and cut her losses. More hours here would only increase her resentment. She wasn't a bitter old hag. Not entirely. But soon she might be if she didn't stop feeling sorry for herself and move on.

4

She squeezed his wrist in apology and strode through the main Vault room, giving half-hearted grins to the patrons who looked at her in pity. She didn't fit in with this crowd. A world she'd once dominated was now foreign. She'd become a pauper in a place where orgasms were currency—at least where receiving was concerned.

When she reached the seclusion of the locker room, defeat set in. She'd come so far from the missionary-position woman she'd been before Lucas. Now she'd fallen from carnal grace. Sex was no longer exciting. Her seven-day-a-week habit had died from starvation, and all she could do was move on. Bury the craving, like she'd buried her husband.

"Goddamn you." She opened her locker door and slammed it shut again. The loud bang reverberated through her, hitting her chest, her heart. The threat of tears returned. Angry, scornful tears making the room blur.

She'd thought she'd done everything right. She hadn't jumped into the Vault experience with gusto. Her steps had been slow. Over unending months, she became the ultimate voyeur, not touching another man until she was ready—mind, body, and soul. Then one after another, the club regulars had failed her, leaving unfulfillment to run rampant, all because her husband's prowess was irreplaceable. "Damn you, Lucas."

"Hey."

She stiffened at the sound of Shay's voice and hoped the woman would let her be. "Can you give me a minute?"

"That depends. Are you going to continue destroying Vault property if I leave you alone?" The sound of softly swishing fabric encroached. "What's going on?"

Pamela inhaled deep and turned to Shay, taking in the beauty of a woman who couldn't possibly understand what was going on in her addled mind.

"You look gorgeous. As always." It was a side-step. An optimistic diversion. Chatting about the seductive red dress

5

clinging to the bartender's breasts and flowing into a sexy skirt at her thighs was better than the alternative.

"Thank you. Leo seems to enjoy the easy access." Shay gave herself a once-over before meeting Pamela's gaze. "Now, spill. What's got you slamming lockers and looking like the world's coming to an end?"

Pamela kept her mouth shut, scared of what would come out if her lips parted. Words built in her throat, clogging the small space, the pressure increasing. Venting wasn't an issue. She could share her hardships with her sister tomorrow. Even her mother, if she was truly desperate. But they didn't fully understand her cravings. Her sexuality. Sharing with Shay, a woman who knew this way of life, would be different. And the thought of having her worst fears confirmed wasn't something she could handle right now.

"Come on, Pamela." Shay stepped forward, her gentle eyes coaxing. "Tell me what's wrong."

The need to purge grew. The truth cut off her air supply until she opened her mouth and words tumbled out. "*Everything*. I can't do this anymore. I need to give up before it kills me."

"Take a deep breath, honey, and tell me what happened."

"Nothing happened." Pamela swung back to her locker, pulled out her loose black skirt, and yanked it up her thighs. "The same nothing that happens every time I come here." She shoved her tank top into the handbag sitting in the back of the locker, unfazed by walking out of here with her lingerie on display. God knew the people dancing upstairs would be wearing far less. "Please tell Leo I want to cancel my membership. You won't see me here again."

"Okay... I can tell him." Shay leaned forward, inching her way into Pamela's sight. "But before I do, can you elaborate? I've seen you with different men, so your comment about 'nothing happening' is throwing me."

"I mean, nothing happens for *me*." She waved a hand to encompass her body—the breasts that never tingled from a man's touch, the pussy that didn't throb in arousal. "In all the time I've been here, and all the men I've slept with, I haven't orgasmed once. Not even a tiny bit. Not even close." She reached for her shoes and dropped the one-inch black heels at her feet. "I'm only kidding myself if I keep coming back."

"Didn't Leo set you up with someone a while ago?" Shay frowned. "Yeah. It was my first night down here, and he was playing the role of instructor. Didn't that work out?"

"That was the first time I'd been with anyone since my husband." She yanked her handbag from the locker and pulled the strap over her shoulder. "I faked my way through it, thinking that was necessary to get into the swing of things. Turns out, I've had to fake it ever since."

Shay slumped onto the bench seat in the middle of the room. "Maybe it's too soon for you to move on."

"It's been three years." For others, the timeline of grief was infinite. Not for her, though. She'd been primed to move on for a long time. "I'm ready. The problem is finding the right person."

"Is there something in particular you're looking for? Is it aesthetic appeal? Are the men not your type? Or do you have a specific kink?"

"I know exactly what I want." A carbon-copy of her husband, at least where the sex was concerned. "I want a man who will take me over and control my pleasure. Someone who knows what I want before I want it and doesn't mistake his cockiness for finesse." She sighed and let her tired shoulders sag as she slumped onto the bench beside Shay. "Sorry for the hysterics. I guess frustration finally has the better of me."

"Is that all it is? Frustration?"

Yes...

Maybe...

7

No.

She stared down at her glossy shoes, the past reliving itself in her mind. "I wasn't married to Lucas for long. We didn't even reach our one-year anniversary. And in that time, he completely changed my sex life. He made me aware of a sexuality I never knew I had. But I didn't realize it was exclusive to our relationship. I thought the physical connection would be replaceable. Maybe not to the exact degree of what we had. I only hoped for something similar. Instead, I'm losing faith in ever finding the part of myself that made me feel most alive."

It sounded pathetic. How could sex be such a significant piece of her? It was only physical exertion, right?

Wrong.

The act was so much more. She needed to be seen without having to wave her arms in the crowd. She wanted to be heard without words. She longed for someone to know her. Yet, she wasn't sure she knew herself anymore.

"Would you trust me to hook you up with a guy who might be able to help?" Shay leaned in and rested her head on Pamela's shoulder.

"I think I'm too far gone. I used to be able to orgasm with the flick of my husband's fingers. Now men need to have mastered the Kama Sutra and bear the scratches of a thousand pleasured virgins before I give them the time of day." She released a half-hearted chuckle. "I'm high maintenance."

"The person I have in mind would see that as a challenge."

"I've been with most of the available men at the Vault."

"You haven't been with him. I'd know." Shay stood and rubbed her hands together. "I have a really good feeling about this. All I need is five minutes to make it happen."

"It's too late. I'm..." An old widow? A born-again virgin? A broken soul?

"In a slump. That's all." Shay started for the door, her face bright with optimism. "And I'm convinced Brute will be the perfect match for you."

CHAPTER TWO

*B*ryan Munro tugged the under-age piece-of-shit through the club by the collar. Standards of Practice could kiss his ass. There was no way he was letting this fucker walk out without being manhandled. If you were cunning enough to pass the bouncer inspection and sneak inside the Shot of Sin nightclub illegally, the last thing you wanted to do was draw attention to yourself by grabbing the first pair of tits that passed your way.

"Come back here and I'll show you what it feels like to be sexually assaulted." He shoved the kid through the open front doors. When the prick righted himself without falling to the pavement, the disappointment was real. "Believe me, some days I miss being in jail. Making you my bitch would bring back memories."

It was a lie. All lies. But the wide eyes of the teen were well worth the pretense.

The bouncer on the door chuckled. "You definitely live up to your nickname, Brute."

"I do." He jerked his chin toward the club. "And if I find

anyone else in there who's underage, you'll find out just how brutal I can be."

The guy straightened. "Sorry, boss."

"You should be." Bryan and his business partners, T.J. and Leo, didn't have time for this lazy bullshit. The adjoining Taste of Sin restaurant was being slammed nightly with eager walk-ins willing to beg for a table when the already extended dining hours couldn't keep up with reservations. And Vault of Sin downstairs always came with a heavy dose of drama. He didn't need Shot of Sin to add legal issues with underage drinkers to his list.

"I'll be more thorough." The bouncer crossed his arms over his chest, his lips thin, his frown deep. A picture of clichéd security.

"Make sure you are." Bryan strode back into the club, his bad luck increasing when he sighted Shay leaning against the entry hall in her tempting thigh-high dress. Leo's girlfriend was not only a thorn in his side, but a fucking pinecone up his ass. If he didn't know better, he'd assume her life's mission was to turn him gray. And she was succeeding. "What do you want, wench?"

Her lips quirked as she pushed from the wall. "I need to borrow your cock for a minute."

He raised a brow and came up beside her, stopping close. "You've finally realized I'm a better option than Leo?"

Her smile turned coy, those long brown eyelashes batting up at him. "Not even close." She pivoted on her toes and sauntered toward the dancing bodies, crooking a finger over her shoulder. "Come on."

He growled and followed, pretending he didn't appreciate the way his sexy subordinate ordered him around. She led him through the thick crowd to the Vault entry, guarded by a lone member of security.

"Why are we going downstairs?" He raised his voice over ·

the thud of music. "I'm supposed to be watching the bar tonight."

"Stop bitching. The staff can do their job without you breathing down their neck for a while." She pulled open the door and disappeared into the darkened stairwell.

He gave the security guard a dubious look and contemplated what lay ahead. The barely controlled twitch of the guy's mouth announced loud and clear that the hell-raiser of the club was likely to shank him with a steel dildo once he was in seclusion. "If I don't come out within twenty minutes, call Leo for help."

"Will do."

Bryan strode inside and pushed the door shut behind him. With the click of the latch, the club music disconnected, the soundproofing replacing the loud beat with static. "Hold up."

The eager way Shay bounced down the steps toward the private sex club increased his apprehension. She was excited about something.

Something that involved his dick.

"Shay," he grated, unmoving. "What's going on?"

She turned to him, the overhead lights shining down on her with a heavenly glow that didn't fool him in the slightest. "There's a woman who needs your help."

"Help? Are we talking about a maintenance problem or a woman-wants-to-get-laid issue?"

He had no problem with the former. The latter was entirely different. Apparently, he'd earned a name for himself within the sordid walls of the club. A name that had him at the front and center of every woman's spank bank.

"This situation leans more toward the latter," she said in a rush. "But hear me out."

He glared. "You know my position on this."

"I know. I know. But this is different. You haven't been

with her before. It won't break any of your precious rules. She's also not the clingy type."

He'd assumed the same about the majority of women who visited the Vault. Unfortunately, he'd been proven wrong time and time again. No matter how brutally honest he was with his intentions, they always expected more from him once he effortlessly pushed them over the line of orgasmic bliss.

"I'm not the helping type. You should ask Leo or T.J."

She shook her head. "I'm not willing to share Leo. And T.J. is far too sweet for this role."

He trudged toward her, the enthusiastic glow in her eyes lessening with each step he took. "*What* role, exactly?"

"I need you to work your magic on someone who's having trouble in the orgasm department."

His frown was an adequate response.

"Don't look at me like it's a hardship." She swung around and continued bounding down the stairs. "Hurry up."

"Wait." Shay knew better than to play matchmaker, which meant curiosity now had him by the balls, pushing him to catch up to her at the bottom landing. He grabbed the crook of her arm and encouraged her to stop. "Why can't someone else handle it?"

"She's tried everyone. Nobody succeeded."

"Then tell her to come back next time the Vault is open. There's always fresh meat to sample."

"She's been attending for months. Probably years. She's ready to cancel her membership."

"Then maybe that's for the best."

Shay's expression morphed from hope to anger. "Don't be such a selfish prick. I know you've got what it takes."

"I don't doubt it. But I'll repeat—I'm not the helping type."

"Then consider it a challenge. Leo told me you have plans

to organize a development night focused on women's pleasure. This would be a great test to your skills."

"I don't need to be tested, sunshine."

"I disagree."

The corner of his lips twitched. "Then drop those panties and allow me to demonstrate."

Her laughter was light and infectious. That was the problem with Shay—she made him feel different, less abrasive, when he much preferred to remain distant and caustic.

"You know that's not going to happen. But I will encourage you to prove yourself with this chick. Every other man here is incapable of making her climax. I'm sure you could outline her problems in some sort of case study and make this the perfect opportunity to show patrons you're fit to teach."

He leaned in, his face inches from hers as he smirked. "I've seen you watching me down here. You know I'm fit to teach."

"Pleasuring innumerable women who are already primed from the Vault atmosphere isn't a valid indication. I doubt you'd have the same results with someone who's highly specific in her needs and no longer wants to be here."

"Highly specific?"

"She wants to be controlled. To be mastered. She doesn't want to draw a road map for every guy who gets between her thighs."

He straightened, trying to fend off the catnip piquing his interest.

She narrowed her eyes and grinned. "Come on. You know you want to. It's a trifecta. You get to pleasure a beautiful woman during work hours. You'll gain a great case-study for your class, while also proving you're the most talented man in the club."

The title wasn't up for debate.

"*Please*." She clasped her hands together and raised them to her chest—begging with an added hint of cleavage persuasion. "Do this for me."

"I won't make any promises. I need to meet her first."

She nodded and walked backward until she reached the locker room doorway. "Bryan, I'd like you to meet Pamela."

Pamela?

Fuck.

He didn't need to step forward to see what she looked like. A gorgeous blonde with ample curves and deep brown eyes. He'd been drawn to her the moment he'd double-clicked the membership photo that slid into his inbox.

Then he'd read her name, and all interest had vanished like condoms at a frat house.

"Brute," Shay warned. "Hurry up and get in here."

He glared as he walked through the doorway and watched the blonde beauty stand from the bench in the middle of the room. Her limited clothing showed off a figure that hadn't changed since her induction. The dark navy corset clung tight, the breast cups supporting a lush chest while the waist curved to promote a perfect hourglass. She met his feral stare momentarily, then just as quickly, she lowered her gaze.

Submission.

Nice.

Usually, the women in the Vault were overly eager. Bright eyes. Visually defiling stares. The type who expected more from him than he ever planned to give. Rarely was there an opportunity to be with someone less enthusiastic. Sometimes it felt like he only had to blink in the wrong direction and the females started to take off their panties.

Not that he could blame them. He had sexual groupies for a good reason.

He cleared his throat, the deep sound a test to how she'd

respond. And just as quickly as her gaze fell, she straightened her shoulders and met him with a narrowed stare, taunting him.

Interesting.

Her defiance conquered the desire to submit.

Maybe she wasn't the easily boxed woman he'd initially thought.

"Have the two of you spoken before?" Shay hovered in the doorway, one shoulder resting against the frame.

"Very little." He'd made sure of it, always happy to distance himself from triggers of his past. "But I processed Ella's application, so I'm familiar with her reasons for being here."

"Pamela," the woman murmured.

He ignored the correction and prowled around the bench seat. From the rebellion in her eyes and the stubborn set to her shoulders, he could tell she wasn't a natural submissive. She wanted the fight. Might even crave it more than the physical pleasure.

"You can leave, Shay." He kept his focus on Ella, taking in the stories her body willingly whispered. She was confident, her posture straight, her chin high and proud. She also came from money. Her shoes were polished and clearly designer. Her corset was made from expensive material, not a cheap knock-off. And her blonde hair was immaculately cut and pulled into a neat ponytail.

"Are you sure?"

"Leave," he grated.

"Pamela?" Shay questioned.

He shot the bartender an incredulous stare. "Leave. *Now*."

She held up her hands in surrender. "I'm going. I'm going."

She muttered something under her breath—an expletive,

he was sure—but he let it slide, choosing to focus on Ella instead.

They stood in silence, a few feet apart, sizing each other up. She was trying to predict his failure before he'd even begun. The added challenge made his pulse increase. There was no excitement in her features. Not even a hint of hope. The walls of pessimism were firmly erected, and he'd take pleasure in knocking them down.

"Shay claims no man can get you off."

Her chin lifted. "That's right."

"I beg to differ."

She scoffed and gripped the strap of her handbag, hitching it higher on her shoulder. "Look, this isn't going to work. We're both wasting our time."

"Why is that?"

She swallowed, fear or manners holding her back.

"You can be honest." He wasn't a pussy who could dish out brutal honesty without taking it in return.

"Really?" She quirked a brow. "In that case, I'm not interested in being with someone driven by arrogance. This isn't a game to me. And I refuse to coddle another guy who thinks he's skilled, when reality would prove he's delusional."

"You think I'm delusional?" Her disinterest was cathartic. A breath of fresh fucking air. Maybe he needed to get Shay to start a rumor about him loving the thrill of the chase. That way women would stop stalking him and he could go back to enjoying his time in the Vault.

"I think you're like everyone else here who expects me to give them a quick thrill and a boost to their ego. I assure you, you'll get neither from me."

Feisty. This woman continued to grow in appeal.

"Look..." She sighed. "I apologize for being rude, but this is pointless." She made for the door. "I'm sorry Shay interrupted whatever you were doing."

"Leaving would be a mistake." He didn't turn to her. He didn't need to. Although she was abrasive, her hope was palpable. "I promise I'll give you what you need, but I won't chase you. You walk out the door and I won't follow."

Her footsteps paused and a deep breath whispered into his ears. "How can you promise that?"

"Because what you interpret as arrogance is actually experience. Unlike other men, I know what I'm doing."

Her wide eyes spoke of silent disbelief. He let her mull it over, predicting a number of responses before she finally spoke.

"A long list of conquests won't help. My appetite is more specific than most."

"Have it your way." He strode for the door, eating up the space between them.

Her throat convulsed. Her fingers twitched. "Wait." She held out a hand, her heated palm connecting with his chest, the delicate touch powerful in its gentleness. "How?"

He quirked a brow. "How?"

Her hand fell and she huffed. "How would you make me come?"

"Chitchat isn't really my thing. Why don't you just let me show you?"

"Because every other man who's received the opportunity has crashed and burned."

"It's not my fault you've had bad taste in lovers."

Her eyes narrowed, the callous slits of spite making his cock twitch. He had her. She may not know it, may not even approve of it, but he'd definitely won.

"Drop the bag." With the jut of his chin, he indicated the leather strap hanging over her shoulder.

She puffed out her chest, and the rebellion spurred his pulse harder. Faster. He was fully invested now, wanting her to continue the game because most women barely tweaked his interest.

"Drop it." His voice was low, the command unmistakable.

She didn't move. Refused to comply.

Silent laughter filled his chest at the obvious way she demanded punishment. Her eyes begged. Her body hummed.

"All right, sweetheart. Have it your way." He encroached, leaning into her. His gaze never wavered as he placed his hand on her upper arm, gliding it over the exposed skin of her shoulder, toward her neck.

He latched onto her throat, her body heat burning his palm. She sucked in a breath, fast and deep, her acquiescence coming in harsh exhalations. Those brilliant eyes sparked before him with flames of annoyance as he held her at his mercy. And still, she didn't back away, didn't even flinch when he tightened his grip.

Any other man might've been put off by her lack of verbal consent. But he didn't care. Not one little bit. He received her permission from the unwavering stare, the lick of her tempting lips, the thrust of her chest.

Her bravado had begun to fracture. It wasn't a large break, merely a fissure to expose how well he'd worked his way under her skin. He wasn't immune either. The increased beat of her carotid against his fingers and the delicate swallow of her throat had his cock twitching against his zipper.

"Drop. It." The words grated from his drying mouth.

She lifted the strap from her shoulder and dropped the weight beside her feet with the clink of loose change.

"Good." He caressed her neck with his thumb and stared into those beseeching eyes. She told him everything he needed to know with that look. She was laid bare. Transparent. "You want this to happen. Want to know how I know?"

Her throat expanded under his palm, her heavy swallow like nirvana through his veins.

He leaned closer, his mouth less than an inch from her ear. "Because I'm listening, Ella. I can hear you. I can read you like a book."

She shook her head. "That's not my name."

He growled at the reminder. "It is tonight."

CHAPTER THREE

*P*amela closed her eyes, sinking into the thrill of the tight grip around her throat. She hadn't had this—the commanding presence, the compelling dominance —in a long time. It filled her with relief, along with other sensations she was truly thankful for. Even if this man did fail to bring her to climax, he'd do it with the slightest achievement.

"Tell me what you like," he whispered.

She stiffened, the hard punch of disappointment hitting her without warning. So much for slight achievements. With the opening of her eyes she was back to square one, not willing to draw a road map.

"Forget it." She shoved at his chest, her hands colliding with unyielding muscle.

He laughed, the humor brightening his harsh features. She didn't care if he could pull off his tailored suit like a *GQ* model, or that his chin-length hair made her itch to run her fingers through it. Hell, she even craved the rough grate of his close-cropped beard against her breasts... But he was a jerk.

A goddamn asshole.

"Move."

He continued to chuckle, the sound fraying her sensitive nerves as she shoved him again. His hands fell, his palms snatching her wrists tight and yanking her into his chest.

"You're touchy," he growled. "All this spite over a rhetorical question."

"It wasn't rhetorical." She tugged in vain to free her wrists.

"Wasn't it? Didn't I just tell you I can read you like a book?" He flashed his teeth.

It wasn't a nice smile. It was vicious. Nasty. And God help her, it made her chest constrict for all the right reasons. Or maybe they were the wrong reasons.

So very, very wrong.

She didn't want to swoon over a guy who could laugh in her face with undiluted smugness. She *shouldn't* swoon over a guy like that. Should she?

"If I were a smart man, I'd pose opportunities for you to show me exactly what you want without asking. Wouldn't I?"

She shook her head in denial. "You're messing with me, and I don't appreciate it."

"Yeah, you do. You're looking for a fight." His fingers pressed into her wrists, his power holding her captive in more ways than one. "That's what you like, isn't it?" His gaze searched hers, back and forth, back and forth, each swipe reading things she didn't want to admit. "Don't tell me other men failed to get such an easy reaction out of you. You're practically shoving what you want in my face."

"Stop it." He was right. So right it hurt. She wasn't usually like this. The need to spar was an anomaly he'd picked up on with flawless precision.

His strong hands turned her around to hitch one arm behind her back, the other forward between her breasts. He pinned her against him, his heated breath brushing her neck.

"I'm only going to say this once," he spoke harshly in her ear. "I don't do safe words. If you want to stop, all you have to do is repeat what you just said and I'm gone. I won't stand here while you kid yourself about your dirty little perversions. If you want me to make you come, you need to own it."

She whimpered. Lucas never made her admit the naughty things running through her mind. He never demanded that of her. To him it was roleplay, a fantasy, while this man made it reality. Being forced to vocalize her desire was torture—punishment of the most delicious kind.

"Tell me you want this." He nuzzled her neck. "Admit you're deliberately pushing because you want me to fight back."

Her heart pounded in her throat. Breathing became an arduous challenge. Her body reacted to him like paper to a flame. She was scorched. Burning. Her edges singed from his affects.

She fought against him, ashamed and achingly aroused as she tried to wrestle her wrists from his grip.

"Good girl." The arrogance tainting his voice made her pussy clench. "I love being right. It makes my dick hard." He proved his point by grinding his cock against her ass.

His large, erect cock.

Damn him. The last thing this accomplished man needed was the asset to back up his ego.

"You're an asshole." She bucked her hips, and his grip tightened to the point of heavenly pain.

"I'm also better than you. At this, I'll *always* be better than you." He nudged her forward, leading her to the lockers. "Put your palms on the metal."

He released her, trapping her between two immovable objects, one devilishly warm, the other chillingly cold. He kept her on her toes. Where had this man come from, and how did he get a cheat sheet on her body?

No. It wasn't her body. It was her mind. He was fucking her from the inside out, his words entrancing her with arousal, his confidence inspiring arrhythmia-inducing hope.

"Put them on the locker, Ella."

She bit her lip and raised her hands, freezing them in place against the metal. There was a heartbeat of silence, the quiet almost deafening when mixed with the rush of blood in her ears.

He lifted her skirt, the hem scratching sensitive skin like sandpaper instead of elegant fabric. Every inch of her responded in erotic fascination—her nipples tightened, her breasts ached, even the hair on the back of her neck rose, eager and greedy for more.

The sensations were foreign. Years had passed since her body had reacted this way. A lifetime.

The smooth graze of his fingers cut across the curve of her bottom, then lower, between her thighs. Slow and torturous.

"You're soaked." His teeth grazed along her shoulder, inspiring a shudder. "But how can that be, sweetheart? I thought you were an ice princess." He nudged aside the crotch of her panties, the slightest brush of her sex sending a wave of pleasure from her core outward. "Turns out you're just as eager for my dick as everyone else."

A hiss of breath escaped her lips. She wanted to hate him. To despise his skill.

The exact opposite happened.

She was indebted to him, her orgasm so frighteningly close she was actually fighting it.

"On second thought, you don't even need my dick, do you?" His derisive chuckle peppered her skin. "I bet I could get you off with one finger."

She closed her eyes, unwilling to admit it would take a lot less.

"Should I prove it?"

A lone fingertip parted her folds, sliding with ease through her arousal. He learned her, trailing inside and out. Back and forth. Around and around. Never penetrating. Only teasing her to the point of silenced hysteria.

He didn't rush, didn't falter in his blissful assault. He was too good, too skilled, and not merely with his touch. His precision came from strategy—a game plan she appreciated whole-heartedly if the lust and adrenaline flooding her veins was anything to go by.

"Enough with the questions." She bucked against him, fighting the mental connection and focusing on the physical. Instantly, she was pushed against the lockers with a responding jerk of his hips. She needed him to do it again, this time with his cock inside her. Over and over. "You talk too much."

"Then I'll stop."

Panic flooded her veins. *Shit*. She wanted his voice. Needed it. The threatening drawl was the cause of her bliss, and she knew he was arrogant enough to withhold it from her. "I take that back. Keep talking... I-I need you to keep talking."

"No, you don't," he whispered into her hair, each word softer than the last.

"I do." She waited long moments, her hips circling to follow the trail of his fingertip. "Please."

Christ, she was begging for sound. Pleading for him.

He didn't respond. Not with words. Only movements. His finger continued to glide around her sex, outlining her pussy lips, then straight down to her core. He circled her opening, painfully slow, deliciously teasing.

She whimpered. Mentally begged.

He felt so good, but she needed the mental stimulation. The dirty words were necessary to get her off.

"Talk to me." She shoved back against his chest. And again, when he didn't answer. "You won't make me come like this."

That finger kept circling, turning her into a liar with the efficient way her orgasm hovered. She shot a pleading glance over her shoulder and their gazes connected in an instant. His confidence washed through her. There was no denying she was in skilled hands. Everything about him hit the right mark.

His touch.

His focus.

His understanding.

He was listening.

Finally, someone was listening. Not to her words, but to *her*.

Pressure slid over her clit, his thumb, the tight press holding the bundle of nerves hostage. A gasp escaped her, and he raised a checkmate brow in response.

Damn him. She turned away, closed her eyes, and rested her forehead against the locker.

His other hand trailed a path around her body, starting at her hip. He drifted over her stomach, through her cleavage, along her sternum to the base of her throat.

Her skin erupted in goose bumps; her lungs tightened. She tilted her head back, offering herself to his mercy. But he didn't take it. He didn't encase her throat in his grip as she wished. Instead, he wove his hand around her neck and fisted her ponytail, pulling tight.

She whimpered.

This man wasn't merely reading her cues and responding, he was taking them a step further. Pushing her. Giving her something she didn't expect.

"Talk to me."

He refused. The only sound came from the upstairs door

opening, the blast of dance music filtering in, before an abrupt disconnect. Footfalls and light chatter echoed forth as he pleasured her. People were approaching, and he showed no intent to stop.

"Whoa." A man's voice carried from the door. "Now this is what I call a proper greeting."

A woman laughed, friendly and light.

Bryan didn't falter. Didn't even pause. He kept her hair in his grip, his finger still teasing her pussy. "Evening," he drawled in greeting. "Look, honey, we've got visitors."

She groaned at the gift of his voice.

Could he tell she enjoyed an audience? She didn't know how or why, but this man had already learned so much about her.

"I said *look*."

Her nipples tingled at his command, and she sucked in a breath to counteract the shock. His words made her sizzle. *No.* She had to keep reminding herself it wasn't the words, it was the conviction in his tone. The pure authority. He spoke with no fear of her rejection. He issued directives he knew she wanted to follow.

"Come on now," he purred. "Play nice."

She whimpered and opened her eyes to see the couple standing a few feet away. The middle-aged woman bit her lip as she nestled close to her companion with a mammoth-sized erection tenting his pants.

Oh, sweet heavens.

Her pussy fluttered, her core clamped down. She panted, no longer capable of speech. The man stared at her, his gaze intent, his appreciation clear while Bryan's lone finger continued to torment her pussy entrance.

"Say hello." There was another tug to her hair, the slight pinch only increasing her pleasure. "Don't be shy."

She moaned and refused with a shake of her head.

Bryan's breathy snicker caused a shudder to flow down her spine. He was loving this, thriving on her defiance.

"Now you're just being rude." His beard grazed the skin of her shoulder, and he tilted her head higher.

"Fuck you," she muttered under her breath.

Fuck me.

Fuck everything.

She became mindless with the hunger for penetration. All she needed was...something. Anything.

"You'd like that, wouldn't you?" He ground his cock into her ass and sank his finger deep into her heat. "You'd fucking love it. Coming all over my dick. Milking me with this tight pussy."

She didn't want to show him how right he was, but her body refused the order. She shuddered, a mere breath away from orgasm. He was so fucking good. *Too* fucking good.

Her core throbbed, over and over, igniting a release she couldn't abate.

"Christ." The word was a breathy exhale. It was relief and pleasure and torture. Closure and rapture and desolation.

Pure, carnal release.

She clawed at the locker and failed to keep herself upright as her pussy contracted, tighter and tighter, clinging to the single digit sheathed inside her. She sank one inch, two, only to be pressed harder against the cold metal, his body helping her stand. Her core spasmed on a continuous loop, one convulsion after another as she panted and gasped for air.

"That's it," he coaxed. "Show me how good I am."

She ground her teeth in defiance, but it was too late. He'd already won. The height of orgasm had been and gone, each contraction now shorter than the last.

Everything became heavy—her arms, her legs, her chest. Relief turned into an uncomfortable tightening beneath her ribs. She'd waited so long. Hope had been fleeting. Now...

now, this smug ass of a man had reignited her libido, and she couldn't be happier.

She turned to face him and tried to ignore the rapid rise of his appeal. They'd been left alone, their audience nowhere in sight as she struggled to regain normal breathing.

"I guess my work here is done." He winked, his fingers fleeing her panties. "And you thought I wouldn't get a quick thrill or a boost to my ego. Turns out I got both."

She let him revel in his victory, wishing the blissful hum of her body wasn't adding fuel to his blazing bonfire of arrogance. He was a jerk. No doubt about it. But Jesus fucking Christ, he was an accomplished jerk.

Her knees buckled and she slid down the cool metal of the lockers, landing in a heap on the floor. Relief overwhelmed her, making her gasps for air turn into gulps for mental stability.

"I'll see you around, Ella." He backtracked, his heated gaze making her self-conscious about her disheveled state before he turned and strode from the room.

She couldn't even find the breath to correct her name. It didn't matter, anyway. He was gone, the upstairs door to the nightclub soon opening and closing with a burst of loud music.

Questions and eager observations filled her adrenaline-fueled mind as she relived what had just happened. He'd opened his own forum in her brain, a mass of squealing groupies pointing out his achievements like they were worthy of Olympic gold.

He hadn't even sought relief. Hadn't even mentioned reciprocation despite the hard, thick length of his erection that had been an unmistakable presence at her ass.

"You good?"

Pamela blinked from her trance and focused on Shay in the doorway.

"Yeah." She cleared the gravel from her throat. "Better than good."

The bartender sauntered forward, her smile wide. "He did great, didn't he?"

Pamela laughed. She couldn't explain it. Couldn't describe it. She didn't think she even wanted to, because the idea of complimenting the arrogant ass was a despised prospect. Then again, he kind of deserved all the praise bubbling in her rapidly flowing bloodstream. She never would've thought an orgasm with minimal penetration was possible. Not even when Lucas had been alive.

All Bryan had needed was one finger.

One. Damn. Finger.

"I'm glad." Shay held out a hand and pulled Pamela to her shaky feet. "Does this mean you won't be canceling your membership?"

She blinked, too shell-shocked to know the right answer. "It means there's hope. And that's enough for now."

CHAPTER FOUR

TWO WEEKS LATER

The shuffle of footsteps at the open office door demanded attention Bryan wasn't enthusiastic to give. "Did you want something?" He met Leo's stare as his friend leaned against the doorframe." Or are you happy to stand there and admire me in silence?"

"What are you up to tonight?"

Bryan raised a brow. "Probably a whole heap of none-of-your-fucking-business. Why?"

"Shay asked if you had plans to play in the Vault."

Great. Another woman to add to the list. "Tell Shay to get a life. I don't want her vetting questions from the vultures down there."

"Christ, you're in a mood. *Again.*"

Bryan sank back in his chair with a huff. He *was* in a mood. This was his night to work the restaurant, and with Taste of Sin now closed, he should already be downstairs relaxing with a beer and a woman. Instead, he battled with annoyance.

He'd finally nutted out the particulars for the development night he would soon run in the Vault. Meticulous detail had gone into the first email to club patrons advising them of what to expect and what they could learn. Yes, he'd expected questions, and yes, there had been many, but all of them had revolved around his sex life and who he'd be fucking in the near future.

"I made the mistake of leaving my phone number on the email I sent to Vault members. Now I've got women hounding my ass. I've had two text me in the last five minutes, asking when I'm coming downstairs."

"Holy shit," Leo exaggerated a whisper. "You poor, defenseless bastard."

Bryan scowled.

"Most men would kill for your position. But not you. For such a hard ass, you really are a pussy when women show any interest."

Yes, he was. A remorseless bachelor for life. He refused to be tied to anyone. Not even temporarily. And if running from commitment-starved women made him a pussy, he'd be happy to wear the title like a badge of honor. "I'm not most men."

"Clearly. But you do realize they'd back off if you settled down with a regular hook-up? If you remain single, they're always going to look for an opportunity."

"I'm not going to let one woman latch her claws for the sake of keeping the rest at bay. They should all know the drill by now. If not, I'll have to give them a reminder."

"Well, it better be friendly. They'll be dripping in their panties if you pull the usual Brute routine." Leo gave a half-hearted laugh. "I don't know how you do it, but they eat up your bad attitude like a vanilla fudge sundae."

That was the vicious cycle. He didn't do nice. Never had.

So, whenever he opened his mouth, the females lapped at his hostile sterility. "Do me a favor and don't mention my routine and vanilla in the same sentence. We both know that's more your style."

"You know what else is my style?" Leo countered. "Committing myself to one woman, so the rest know I'm off-limits."

"Everyone knows you're off-limits because Shay threatens to slash them with a broken bottle if they get within two feet."

"Yep." Leo grinned. "She's a keeper." He pushed from the doorframe, making way for the person who entered.

Shit. Janeane. She was one of the text-message hounds. Long brown hair, dark hazel eyes, a body made for sin, and a determination for commitment that made his skin crawl.

"Looks like you've got a visitor," Leo drawled. "I'll leave you two alone."

"You need to hang around." Bryan narrowed his gaze on his business partner, relaying an unmistakable message. "We still have things to discuss."

His friend grinned in return. "I'd love to, buddy, but I'm going to be busy helping my girlfriend get a life. We'll catch up later." Leo gave a salute in farewell, then disappeared down the hall.

Fucker.

"He was in a hurry." Janeane sauntered toward the desk, her hips moving with an exaggerated sway. "How you doin', Brute?"

"Fine." He gripped the armrests on his chair, holding his temper at bay. "You?"

"Good."

He understood the look she gave him. It was siphoning. She was trying to get more sex out of him and wouldn't succeed. He'd already slept with her once. That was the extent of their tally—past, present, and future. "What are you doing up here?"

"I thought we could discuss your upcoming development class. Do you still want me to be your assistant?"

He thought it over. After her text messages, and now the visit into the staff area of the club, he knew he should find someone else. But who? She was a carbon copy of every other woman in the Vault. Once he slept with them, his sperm became a potent commitment supplement making them rabid for more.

He really needed to figure out how to get that shit fixed.

"It's not an assistant, as such." He leaned back in his chair, relaxed, a picture of disinterest. "I only need someone to demonstrate on."

"Then I'm your girl."

Of course, she was.

"But I'd prefer to practice first." She raised the hem of her skirt and started lowering her underwear.

"No need." He pushed to his feet and strode around the desk. "I want the session unscripted."

She batted her lashes and dropped her G-string to the floor. "No problem. Tonight can be just for fun."

"Not interested."

She slid forward and placed her hands on his chest. "Are you sure?" Her nails grazed a trail down his pecs, over his stomach, to his crotch. "I bet I can convince you."

He'd happily take that wager. He'd even stake his house on it. "You won't win." He eyed her with apathy, knowing his flaccid cock was incapable of resurrection under her grip. He wasn't interested. At all. And if she needed to grope him to get the picture, so be it.

"You're not in the mood tonight?" She pouted. "What's wrong?"

"You know I'm not a repeat offender, Janeane. We won't sleep together again."

Her palm paused on his cock, her brows knit tight. "But the class you're teaching…"

"Is a one-off. It's business. If you want to fuck, go downstairs and find someone else."

Her hand fell away. "I thought—"

"You thought wrong." He didn't want an affiliation with any woman. And he definitely didn't want her to latch her claws any deeper into the assumption that they had something between them. "I suggest you go back downstairs and find a guy who can treat you right."

Her lips kicked in another vain attempt at seduction. "I think we both know that's not how I want to be treated."

Jesus Christ. For the love of promiscuity. He raked a rough hand over his beard, his fingers digging deep when his phone beeped again. This shit had to stop.

Janeane licked her lips, ignorant to the underlying tension in the room. "Come on, Brute. Do what you want with me."

He cocked a brow. "You sure that's what you want?"

"You know it is." Her eyes brightened.

"Okay, then." He gently grabbed her wrist and led her into the hall. "I'll see you later."

Her mouth gaped as he dropped his hold and inched back to slam the door in her face. *Perfect.* Peace and fucking quiet.

"*Brute.*" She banged on the door.

"For fuck's sake." He clenched his teeth. What did he have to do to stop these women from praising the ground he walked on? It was no secret he treated them with contempt. Apart from telling them to fuck off, he'd exhausted all other forms of rejection. But still, they came at him like defensive linebackers on a quarterback. "Unless you're looking for your underwear, you need to leave."

She huffed. "Fine. Keep them as a souvenir."

"Yeah, thanks." He picked the scant piece of material off the floor and threw it in the trash. He didn't need a reminder. She had his fucking phone number and he was sure she wouldn't let him forget.

"Bye, Brute."

He closed his eyes with a sigh. "Bye, Janeane."

Peaceful silence followed, and he welcomed it with building annoyance. The Vault was supposed to be his sanctuary. His domain. He owned the ground it was built on. Literally. He'd spent years cultivating the perfect environment for his gratification, only now, fucking had become a chore. There was no thrill. No chase. Most importantly, there was no respect.

Sex outside of the club wasn't an option. He wouldn't date, and he refused to waste time searching for women morally capable of enjoying an uninhibited one-night stand. He didn't have the patience or the motivation. Instead, he'd had to settle on growing the list of rejected women inside the Vault. The ones who kept coming back for more. Over and over. Without remorse or dejection.

That shit wasn't admirable. And it definitely wasn't attractive. The more a woman chased him, the less respect he gave her in an effort to put her off his scent. Even then, his form of rejection seemed to smell like the latest best-selling fragrance to hit the market.

He couldn't fucking win.

"This is bullshit." He yanked open the filing cabinet and sorted unorganized invoices to distract himself from where he wanted to be. Where he *should* be.

Another slicing beep sounded from his phone, and he slammed the cabinet shut in frustration. He pulled the cell from his pocket, the grind of his teeth harsh enough to cause damage. He'd turn the fucking thing off until morning. Then he'd get the number changed.

He was poised to shut down the device when it started to vibrate, the screen changing with an incoming call from an unknown number. His teeth should've cracked under the weight of his rage.

"If this is another woman..." He pressed connect, his nostrils flaring as he placed the device at his ear. "*What?*"

There was a beat of silence. A delicious beat where he hoped he'd given the caller enough reason to change their mind about asking him to hook up. Or fuck. Or whatever version of a proposition they wanted to use.

"Bryan?"

Yep. Another fucking woman. "Who's this?"

"It's Tera."

Tera?

He frowned. He only knew one woman by that name, and he had less enthusiasm to speak to her than he did with the scavengers at the Vault.

"Bryan?" Her voice was timid, less forthright than he remembered.

He ran a hand over his mouth and contemplated hanging up. "Yeah."

"It's your cousin, Tera." She paused, probably expecting him to spread a welcome mat. The poor thing would be waiting a while. "Is this a good time to talk?"

He scoffed. How the fuck did he answer that? Was now a good time? Really? Was now, more than ten years after being cut from the family, a good time to talk?

"Sure." He didn't hide his animosity. "I've been hanging out for the perfect opportunity to catch up. Who knew it would be a random Saturday night, a lifetime after you all turned your backs on me?"

"Bryan..."

"Don't fucking *Bryan* me. Tell me why you called so we can get this over with."

She sighed. "I called to ask you to come home."

"Not going to happen."

"Not even if your mom is sick?"

The rage disappeared. The bitterness, too. The world stopped. The sound of the club and the echo of his heartbeat pausing along with it. He thought this day would never come. That his family would always treat him like a pariah—unworthy of their attention. After a childhood chasing parents who tried to ignore his existence, he had finally been acknowledged.

"Bryan, are you still there?"

"I'm here." He leaned against the filing cabinet, contemplating the need to hang up. He didn't want to know. He didn't want to care.

"I'm sorry to be the one to tell you this, but she has terminal cancer."

Fuck. He'd wondered if this outcome would ever eventuate from his mother. Not the karma that reared its head in the form of a disease with a death sentence. He'd always wondered about the regret—the moment she would realize she had a list of sins she needed to absolve before she passed into whatever holy land she thought was waiting for her.

"She's been fighting for a while now. I'm just not sure how much she has left in her."

A while. He really shouldn't be surprised. "If she wants to see me, she can call herself."

"She doesn't even know I've called." The words hung like a noose awaiting an unwilling neck. "Nobody does."

In other words—they still didn't care about him. Nobody did.

He gave a derisive laugh. The possibility of death hadn't even inspired affection in his mom. Why, after all this time, did he expect something different from the stone-cold bitch?

"Thanks for the call, Tera."

"Are you going to come home?" she asked in a rush.

"Tampa was never my home. My parents made sure of that." He cleared his throat and tried to clear his mind of the past at the same time. "It's best for everyone involved if you lose this number."

He waited for an acknowledgment of his request—the slight hitch in her breath—before he disconnected the call and pocketed his cell.

He didn't have a home. Didn't need or want one.

He had a refuge, though, and it was time he reclaimed it.

CHAPTER FIVE

*P*amela handed her identification to the security guard at the parking lot entrance to the Vault. She was buzzing, every inch of her alive with possibility.

The last two weeks had been spent reliving what had happened the last time the secret part of the club was in session. The awakening. The pleasure. The pure ease with which she'd come undone under a skillful hand.

"Have a good night." The guard returned her ID and indicated for her to go ahead with a jerk of his chin.

"Thank you." She hitched her handbag higher on her shoulder and approached the darkened stairwell. The sound of moans and grunts became louder the farther she descended, until she was at the bottom step, peeking inside the Vault.

For once, she smiled as she strode by the bar, no longer frustrated at the ease with which women were getting their rocks off. She did the customary disrobe in the locker room, packed away her handbag, and then returned to the main area.

The room held the usual patronage, apart from a few

unfamiliar faces who didn't pique her interest. Couples mingled with drinks in their hands, others fucked in quiet corners or blatant positions on sofas.

Nobody paid her much attention. No more or less than usual.

"Pamela," Shay called from behind the bar. "You're back."

"Yeah." She approached the grinning woman and slid onto a vacant stool. "I thought I'd give this another try after the success from the last session."

"I'm glad to hear it. Can I get you a drink to celebrate?"

"Sure. Tequila sunrise, please."

Shay made the concoction while Pamela swiveled on her seat, scoping the crowd. There was nothing new or different about the scene before her. One couple used the sex swing. Singles crowded the open doorways to the adjoining rooms. Some regrouped around the bar.

The only thing missing was her resentment.

"He's not here yet."

She turned to Shay and grasped the drink now placed in front of her. "Who? Brute?"

"Isn't that who you came back for?"

"No." It was the truth. "I have no misconceptions about being with him again." She didn't want to fuel his ego, no matter how skillful those hands were. "Not that I was technically with him in the first place. All it took was a thumb, a fingertip, and some smoothly drawled words."

What made her sashay her butt back to the Vault was the hope that Bryan had opened the floodgates when he'd broken the drought. Hopefully, whoever she decided to play with next would be just as successful.

"That sounds about right." Shay chuckled. "I swear he was born with a gift. He always leaves women begging for more."

"I wish I didn't agree." Unfortunately, she did. He was

41

truly skilled in the art of pleasure. And undeniably undeserving of his talent.

"Then why not try for another round? If you technically weren't together last time, it wouldn't go against his hook-up rules."

"Rules? Really?" Incredulity dripped from her lips. The contrast from his technique to his temperament continued to shock and amaze her. "No, thanks. God knows I wouldn't want to step on his toes."

"He's not that bad. Honestly. I wouldn't have encouraged him to help you out if he was. He knows what he wants the same way you do. The difference is, he never wavers."

"Tell me about it." Pamela took a gulp of her drink. "I wavered like a palm tree in a cyclone. There isn't a guy here who I didn't at least flirt with, all in the name of trying to get a fix."

Shay placed her hands on the bar and gave a sad smile. "Then, honey, can you really blame him for setting firm boundaries? At least women know what to expect from him."

True. Maybe she shouldn't blame Bryan for owning his shit. Self-empowerment and all that pompom shaking stuff. "I guess. Doesn't stop his personality rubbing me the wrong way."

"Who gives a shit which way his personality rubs you as long as those orgasms keep coming? Believe me, if Leo would let me bag and gag every guy who walked in here so there was no annoying small talk—"

A guy sitting two stools down cleared his throat, drawing their attention.

"Oh, come on, Jeff. Don't tell me you're not sporting wood at the thought of being bagged and gagged."

The guy grinned. "Get me a bourbon and dry, and I'll pretend I didn't hear a word."

Shay chuckled as she grabbed the requested liquor

bottle. "See? Bag and gag is definitely the answer. But it's not going to happen. This is a sex club, not a bonding retreat, and you pay good money to get in those doors. Make the most of it. Hit him up for a full round. What's the worst he could do?"

Maybe Shay was right. Pamela's decision should revolve around Bryan's skills, not his attitude. "I'll think about it."

"Well, think quick." Shay focused over Pamela's shoulder. "Because the man of the moment has arrived."

The pound of her irregular heartbeat echoed in her ears, the reaction bringing an unhealthy dose of confusion.

She swiveled on her stool and captured the man in her sights. His suit covered him like armor, strong and sure. His shirt was white and crisp, with a gleaming black tie hanging loose around his neck. He must be working, not playing. Otherwise, he'd be in boxers or briefs, as the Vault rules stated.

She grasped her glass, keeping her hands busy while her mind worked overtime. Asshole or not, he'd been blessed with physical appeal. The type that hadn't lessened since learning more about his personality.

His expression wasn't welcoming in the slightest. His eyes were harsh, his face covered in a light, bristly beard that always seemed impeccably trimmed. He had strong shoulders, a solid frame, and a powerful stride.

An emotionless vortex from head to toe.

A shuddering thrill worked through her without permission. She didn't want to be attracted to him. Hell, she'd drink herself under the table in the hopes her sober goggles were adversely affected with a few shots, but the alcohol wouldn't help.

She was intrigued by him.

Attracted, intrigued, and maybe a little curious, too.

"I might go and ask what his plans are." She spoke aloud,

hoping it formed some sort of commitment with the universe to stop her from backing out.

He continued toward one of the side rooms, his focus hitting her with a scowl.

She paused, caught halfway off her seat.

She waited for a sign. A spark. An acknowledgment of the monumental zing they'd shared last time she was here.

Nothing.

He glanced away without so much as a twitch to his lips.

"Umm." She turned back to the bar. "That didn't seem friendly."

"That's Brute. One hundred percent asshole, one hundred percent of the time. Doesn't stop him from fucking like a Trojan."

Damn it. Body parts reacted without warning—breasts, tummy, and lower. *Deeper*. When had she become a sucker for punishment?

She chanced another glance over her shoulder and focused on the darkness of the room he'd disappeared into. She didn't want to give this brutal man any power over her, but the truth was, he already had it. He could give her things no other man seemed capable of.

"I assure you, he does know how to have fun. He's just extremely picky about who he lets past his defenses."

A loner.

Like her husband.

The familiarity softened her interest a little. Not enough. The past seemed to repeat itself, and like with her husband, she found herself unable to walk away.

"Are you going to chicken out?" Shay's voice was light, a bare whisper of subconscious thought through Pamela's frazzled mind.

"No. It's all good. I'll go see what he's up to. There's no

harm in asking, right?" She sucked hard on her straw, finishing her drink. "Wish me luck."

"Go get 'em."

Pamela gave a chuckle in farewell and slid from her stool, righting her favorite deep-pink corset as she padded in his direction. This situation would be different if he weren't the only man standing after years of unreachable orgasms.

He was a unicorn. That was all.

A vicious, snarling anomaly.

And if she wanted to be brutally honest with herself, she wasn't entirely enthusiastic about propositioning previous play partners. The possibility of repeating the mistakes of her past made her skin crawl.

She stopped in the doorway, taking in the shadowed sight of him as he leaned against the wall, staring at the threesome kissing and caressing on the circular bed in the middle of the room. The appeal of Zoe and her men had always drawn Pamela's attention. Not tonight, though. Right now, she couldn't stop staring at the man who owned her pleasure. The man who made her pussy clench with remembrance.

Damn him.

She came to his side, ignoring the deep, woodsy scent of his aftershave wrapping its potion around her. "Hey."

Ten children could have been conceived in the time it took his gaze to finally meet hers. There were no words. No familiarity or friendship. Only obligation bleached of warmth as he jutted his chin. Not only a cold shoulder, but a cold stare.

Problem was, she was here now, by his side, and she didn't want to walk away with her tail between her legs. Especially not when Shay's words repeated in her head, mantra-style—*doesn't stop him from fucking like a Trojan.*

"Are you working?" She fought to remain detached. "You're still wearing your suit."

"Just finished."

His tone carried a hint of "fuck off." A hint she should take. She should grasp the warning and stride from the room. From the club. From his life. Instead, she let her focus wander along the strong lines of his chest, down to the thick thighs she could still remember pressed against her.

Curse him for being a tease to her starved ovaries.

Those hands had inspired daydreams capable of lasting months. Those legs had helped stabilize her during the most tumultuous orgasm.

He pushed from the wall and walked by her without so much as a farewell.

"Hey." She frowned at his retreating back. "Hold up."

He stopped, his shoulders broad and menacing.

"Are you interested in playing tonight?"

This time the beat of silence rang in her ears like an exploding bombshell. The world collectively held its breath.

Slowly, he turned to face her, the furrow between his brows sharp enough to cut stone. "Have I done anything in the last five minutes to give you the impression I'm interested?"

"Uh..." Her throat dried, cutting off her words.

"The answer you're looking for is no," he muttered under his breath. "I didn't say hello. I didn't even smile. Then I *fucking walked away*. What more do I have to do?"

Shock addled her brain, making coherence impossible. She didn't know whether to apologize or lash out. Whimper or snarl. She'd been in this situation before. Many times. But always in reverse. She'd never been accused of not taking a hint. She was always the accuser. Difference was, she wasn't such an ass about it. "A simple 'no' would've sufficed."

"Then, 'no.'" He raised his voice and his arms at the same time, drawing attention. "I'm not interested."

She blinked on rapid repeat, trying to remain strong while

46

humiliation burned her cheeks. "You're a rude son-of-a-bitch."

She walked past him, unwilling to let him get his belittling fix.

"Hold up." The command reverberated off the walls, stopping orgasms, pausing foreplay. Her cheeks heated as more than one inquisitive stare turned toward them. "*I'm* a son-of-a-bitch?"

Panic clogged her throat. She was confident. Empowered. But up against a man like Brute, her self-worth flickered, threatening to snuff completely.

"That's enough," Zoe's voice carried from the bed. "Whatever this is, it doesn't need to be shared in front of a crowd. Brute, you should know better."

No, Pamela should've known better. She should've listened to her gut and left well-enough alone. Before resentment settled in. Before she'd turned to Shay for help. And definitely before this thug had entered the picture.

"I'm not the only one who should know better." Bryan strode by her. "Ignorance to the club rules is becoming an epidemic down here."

He entered the main area with his smooth gait still intact. Each step he took promoted his control, his self-worth, while her resilience to stand tall teetered on a precarious edge.

This could've been worse. At least he'd confined her humiliation to a small room and a minimal number of witnesses. He could have—

"I shouldn't need to remind everyone in attendance that no means fucking no." He demanded the attention of the entire club with a raised voice. "You take rejection without pause or you get the fuck out of my club. Are we clear?"

Her lips parted, her mortification spilling out with a ragged breath.

There were no words to describe the carnage of his

attack. He was deliberately ostracizing her. For what? Because she'd asked him to play?

"You all received my email earlier in the week," he continued. "And I'm fucking pissed that a lot of you took it upon yourself to use my cell number as your personal booty call."

She glanced around, expecting condemnation and judgment. What she found was the same discomfort staring back at him from numerous women. Some looked abashed, others appeared confronted, while men ping-ponged their attention around the Vault trying to determine who'd triggered the earthquake.

Bryan glared, taking the time to pinpoint every female in sight. "That shit has to stop. We have strict rules in place for a reason, and I'll be damned if I'm made to feel pestered in my own club. Respect boundaries and take non-verbal cues or expect to have your membership canceled." He sucked in a breath and let it out with force. "And if I find out anyone has a cell phone in here instead of keeping it secure in the locker room, there's going to be hell to pay."

The silence thickened.

"Thanks for the reminder," Leo called from the bar, a hint of amusement in his voice. "Who wants a drink?"

As quickly as the wildfire had spread, the flames were doused under the offer of alcohol. Couples returned to their canoodling, voyeurs assumed their positions, and exhibitionists sank back into bliss.

The world began to revolve again, circling around her while her feet remained in place.

"I wouldn't take it to heart." Zoe came to stand beside her, the gorgeous woman's brows pinched. "From the whispers I've heard tonight, the outburst was inevitable."

"I...um." Lost for words? Really? The effect of this man had no bounds. She still had no clue what had just happened.

"I'm sure it wasn't supposed to be directed at you." Zoe narrowed her gaze. "Unless you've been calling and texting him to hook up."

"No. *God*, no." If it wasn't for his magic touch, she wouldn't have given him the time of day. "I wouldn't be that stupid."

"You'd be surprised how many women are. I've heard whispers that there's a bet over who can sleep with him next. The members involved aren't shy about it. They're all trying to be the lucky lady who takes him off the market."

"As far as I'm concerned, he's all theirs." The rhythmic sounds of sex and fulfillment built as if they had never stopped. "I just wish I didn't feel like such an idiot." She *had* pestered him and hadn't taken his not-so-subtle cues. "I should've paid more attention to his demeanor."

"Brute's demeanor?" Zoe laughed. "If we all did that, nobody would ever talk to him."

"I guess." She nodded, trying to appreciate the camaraderie even though acid ate through her stomach. "I better get going."

"You can't go now." Zoe turned to the men on the bed and raised a splayed hand, asking for five minutes. "If you leave, his shitty attitude wins. Let's get a drink first."

She wasn't interested in claiming any sort of victory. Besides, she couldn't fight someone who was striding from the room. "No, I've reached my limit." Of bullshit *and* alcohol. "Don't leave your guys waiting."

"Honey, they're not going anywhere."

"Maybe not, but I am. I can't stay here. Thanks for the offer, though."

She didn't say goodbye. Not to Zoe, Shay, or a single soul as she slinked her way through the main room, the newbie lounge, and the entrance hall. She had to get out of there before her head exploded from the vacuum to her pride.

CHAPTER SIX

*B*ryan had his hand in the safe, reaching for his keys, wallet, and cell, when the office door flung open, only to be slammed shut seconds later.

"What the fuck is wrong with you?" Shay came up behind him, a solidified form of indignation and fury.

"The Vault was getting way out of hand. It's time I pulled everyone back into line. I'm not going to apologize for reminding them of the rules."

"I'm not talking about that. I want to know why the hell you would make an example of Pamela when she did nothing wrong."

He winced. That name. It fucking killed him. Every time. "Nothing wrong?" The question came through clenched teeth. "How about calling me a son-of-a-bitch for declining a hook-up?"

"I don't care if she forcibly tried to give you an anal exam. You could've let her down gently. There was no need to make a fool out of her."

"Mind your own business, Shay."

He didn't regret a second of his anger tonight. Especially

after he'd been stopped in the Vault stairwell and told about the group of women who had started placing bets on his sex life. That knowledge had been enough to send him nuclear.

The only saving grace was their luck at choosing him as a target. If another man, or woman, for that matter, had been treated this way, he would've gone postal long ago.

"It is my business, seeing as though I was the one who convinced her to speak to you."

His chest tightened, the unmistakable beat of rage clogging his throat. "You told her to hassle me?"

"Hassle you?" She cocked her hips. "She didn't even want to go near you. I had to talk her into it."

He should've known Shay was a part of this. Should've fucking known. "Then you're to blame. Not me. I made it obvious I wasn't interested. I barely said two words to her before walking away. She was the one who followed *me*. She's the one who continued to act like I was a sure thing because, apparently, she got the wrong impression from you."

Her posture shifted, the slightest sign of guilt.

Just because Ella wasn't as forthright as the others who had called or texted, didn't mean she wouldn't be the next time the Vault opened. His announcement had been a caution to every patron who needed to be reminded that hints of rejection were to be taken as seriously as blatant refusals.

"And like I said downstairs, she's not the only one." He lobbed his cell toward her, the device fumbling in her fingers before coming to rest in her grip. "Check the messages. See just how many women from the Vault are trying to ride my dick."

"I don't—"

"*Fucking look.*" He didn't care if she thought he was irredeemable. But he sure as shit wouldn't have her thinking the women down there were all sweet and virtuous.

51

She raised a haughty brow and cocked a hip as she unlocked his screen and navigated to the texts. She scrolled and scrolled, her eyes skimming messages he knew were as vulgar as they were annoying.

"Your girl may not have been a serial offender. But it was only a matter of time."

"She's not like that... Holy shit, I can't believe Elise sent you a nude selfie."

He nodded. Elise had a fine rack, but he would still delete the pic and place her firmly on his shit list. "One of many."

She winced and handed over the phone. "It doesn't mean you have the right to take your frustration out on Pamela. Her involvement was my fault."

"Shay admitting guilt?" He pocketed his cell, along with his keys and wallet. "You must really like this woman."

"I feel sorry for her. She's too young to be a widow."

He'd almost forgotten about the dead husband. Didn't matter, though. The only thing worse than a pushy woman was a pushy woman with baggage. "She's attractive, and new men continue to join the Vault. She'll find someone to suit her soon enough."

There was no doubt. Apart from her beauty, she was passionate and sexual. The top three checkboxes on any hot-blooded male's list.

"And what about you?" Shay crossed her arms over her chest. "After your demeaning display, I think you're going to find it hard to get laid in the Vault. Female solidarity can be a bitch."

"Female solidarity can kiss my ass. It's my club. If I want to wipe the slate clean of women members and start fresh, I will." Culling members seemed like a damn good idea.

"You're not the only one who owns the club. It's Leo and T.J.'s, too."

He growled, his teeth clenched tight. He loved this

woman. Really, he did. But holy fuck, he hated her at times. "Tell Leo I'm leaving."

"I don't think—"

He held up a hand. "When it comes to me, don't think. Ever again. You hear me? Stay out of my sex life unless you want me meddling with yours."

Her chin hitched, the expression held for a brief second before she nodded.

"I'm glad we're finally on the same page."

Those arms remained locked tight over her chest as he walked from the office.

He strode into the hall and down the stairs to the bar. The club was in full swing with loud music and a packed dance floor. His peripheral vision caught sight of the opening Vault door, and he paused to make sure he didn't have to hide in the crowd to save himself from another female leech.

The guard manning the entrance stepped aside to welcome someone from the darkness.

Bryan should've kept walking. Should've gone straight to the parking lot without giving a fuck about anyone from the private club. But then it was too late. Ella strode from the shadows, wearing a silky dress barely covering the scant lingerie beneath.

She gave a half-hearted smile to the guard, then worked her way across the dance floor, heading toward the main entrance to Shot of Sin.

"You can't let her walk out on her own." Shay's raised voice came from over his shoulder, having the effect of a surprise enema.

"I'm on it."

There was a reason they'd renovated the Vault to have a parking lot exit. Escaping through a mass of drunken revelers at the front of the club wasn't an option, especially for a woman on her own. She'd have to walk around the building unattended. Unprotected.

"Goddamn it." These women would be the death of him. Or at least his libido. He turned to face Shay. "Go back downstairs. I'll make sure she gets to her car."

"Will you make sure she gets an apology, too?"

He scowled. *Apology, my ass.* "Good night, Shay."

She smiled, big and wide and full of spite. "Night, Brute."

Finding Ella again wasn't hard. She parted the sea of pussy-starved men with a whiplash effect. He followed, hanging back at least ten feet. He wouldn't talk to her. She wouldn't even know he was there. All he would do was shadow her to her car and kiss her annoyance goodbye once she safely drove away.

She reached the club doors, tipped her head so she didn't make eye contact with the bouncer, and walked into the night.

He did the same, approaching Greg a few seconds after.

"Everything okay, boss?"

"Yeah. Heading home." They both stared after Ella.

"A friend of yours?"

"No, she's from downstairs."

Greg nodded, lowering his attention to her swaying ass.

Nobody inside the club knew what lurked behind the guarded Vault of Sin doors. Not the bouncers, not the Shot of Sin staff, and definitely not the crowd who continued to carve up the dance floor on a weekly basis. There was only Bryan and his business partners, along with very minimal bar staff. To everyone else, it was an exclusive VIP area, with the people coming in and out carrying the intrigue of celebrity status.

"Keep your eyes on the door," he growled. "I'll make sure she gets to her car."

"Sure thing."

Ella gained distance, and two men waiting in the crowded line for a cab stepped back to follow her along the building. They framed her, leaning close, making their intentions known as Bryan lengthened his stride.

To her credit, she didn't slink away. She stopped, faced one of the men with a jut of her chin, and announced loud enough for everyone to hear, "I'm not interested."

He could've laughed at the parallels of their earlier situation. Then again, it made him think of the differences, too.

Her position contained vulnerability. His hadn't.

She needed to use aggression to get them to back off. He'd merely done it to cause a scene.

The men took the rejection, chuckling to themselves as they made their way to the end of the cab line. Bryan slowed, waiting to overhear a derogatory comment, a snide remark, anything to give him the justification to break a nose or crack a jaw.

Nothing came.

The men were harmless as well as tactless.

Ella continued along the building, her heels tapping with her sure stride. Once she turned the corner of the building she'd be out of sight from club security. From anyone. Except those who thought it might be a good idea to follow a gorgeous woman into a private parking lot in the early hours of the morning.

With a quick glance over her shoulder, she took a hard left and disappeared from view.

She hadn't seen him. Hadn't paid enough attention to her surroundings to notice he'd followed. Her main focus was on the cab line and the men who had approached her.

Big mistake.

She needed to pay more attention.

He increased his pace, wanting to make sure nobody

waited in the darkness. Once he turned the corner, his feet hit the gravel of the parking lot. The crunch beneath his soles was unmistakable.

She heard it, too, if the way she gripped her handbag and riffled through the contents was any indication.

Fuck.

If she turned, he'd have to talk to her. And if she didn't, he'd be stuck with the guilt of knowing he'd unintentionally scared her. Maybe he should call out. Say a quick, "Hey, you fucking idiot, why didn't you use the other exit?"

But he didn't want to speak to her again tonight. Or anyone else, for that matter. The thought of socializing had the appeal of a drug-free circumcision. Not that the feeling was a stretch from any other moment when he had to be chatty.

He ignored the crunch of his footsteps and followed, closing in on her. His pace hadn't increased. Hers had slowed. Why the hell had she slowed?

He was about to announce his presence in an effort to ease her fears, when she swung around, raising a pocket knife in his direction.

Her lips parted at the sight of him, the determined squint of her eyes changing to a widened stare of confusion.

"You plan on using that?" He focused on the knife, the blade barely long enough to cause significant damage. Didn't stop her from squinting at him as if planning the best way to slash and dash. "The Vault has an exit to the parking lot for a reason. You shouldn't be out here on your own."

Her cheeks darkened, in embarrassment or anger, he wasn't sure. But she kept wielding that knife like she had every intention of using it. "You followed me all this way to give me a lecture?"

"I followed you to make sure you got to your car safely."

She scoffed, closing the knife with a confident flick

before throwing it back into her handbag. "Chivalry doesn't suit you. It doesn't even make sense, seeing as though you're the reason I felt too humiliated to walk back through the Vault."

The pang in his chest wasn't appreciated.

"Go back inside." She swiveled on the toes of her shiny black shoes and continued along the building. "I don't need your help."

She walked away from him, striding in the opposite direction when every other woman seemed to salivate over the ability to have a conversation with him. Maybe Shay was right. This woman might not be a leech after all.

"That wasn't the case two weeks ago." His retort came from left-field. An unscripted retaliation he didn't see coming.

She kept walking. One step. Two. Then she gifted him with another swirl, rounding on him, spitting contempt in his direction. "You know what?" She snapped her lips closed.

"What? Let me have it." He shouldn't have found her fury humorous. "Get it off your chest, princess."

Her eyes flared. "Oh, buddy, I don't know where you get off speaking to me like that when I've done nothing wrong. Tonight, you treated me like I was trying to tattoo myself on your charcoal-riddled soul, or steal your cherished bachelorhood."

She stepped forward, straightening her shoulders. Women really needed to get a clue that thrusting their breasts didn't work in their favor. It only made men feel like they'd scored a triple-point bonus during battle.

"Let me assure you," she spat, "I'm not interested in either. In fact, if you were the last man on Earth, I'm pretty sure I'd start fucking livestock to get my kicks just so I didn't have to deal with your bullshit attitude." Her mouth remained open, gaping a little.

Yeah, sweetheart, your diatribe did include a reference to bestiality.

"Good to know." His lips kicked into a smile, and the flare of her nostrils announced she didn't appreciate it.

"This isn't funny."

No, it wasn't. Apart from the enjoyment he received from her annoyance, this wasn't funny at all. He didn't like having his enjoyment of the Vault washed out from underneath him by disrespectful women. He didn't like being railroaded. And he certainly didn't like the reminder that he had a family back in Tampa, ignoring his existence. "No, you're right. After the day I've had, your lack of interest is a fucking relief."

"Well," she grated, walking away, "I'm glad I could ease the tension."

He didn't follow this time. The nagging throb in his chest increased. It wasn't his fault she'd been caught in the line of fire earlier. She'd been collateral damage. A tiny blip on the casualty radar.

All he'd done was announce his disinterest. Loudly. While deliberately drawing the attention of other club patrons.

Fuck.

"I had a shit of a day, okay? I shouldn't have taken it out on you."

She froze, her back still turned. "Was that an apology?"

If it was, it was a shitty one, but coming from him, it was the holy grail of remorse. "It's whatever you need it to be."

She released a sardonic laugh and pounded out the distance to the end of the building.

The ache beneath his ribs grew, demanding more. More what? He didn't know.

"Look, I shouldn't have directed my rant at you." He jogged to catch up, chasing the wanted distraction.

"So you don't regret what you said, just that you included

me in it?" She approached the line of cars and slipped between a polished SUV and T.J.'s new BMW.

"Hell, no, I don't regret it. It was a long time coming." He followed her into the small space and stopped a foot away, at the start of her door. "You don't think I have a right to tell women to back off? If it was your private number being distributed around the club and guys started texting at all hours, asking to hook up, while also sending unsolicited dick pics, I'd make sure those fuckers never stepped foot in the club again. Yet, when it happens to me, I'm supposed to be happy about it? Come on. Cut me a break. I enjoy unwanted attention as much as you do."

She opened her door and he retreated a step, not realizing how close they'd become.

"Tell me, Ella. Don't I deserve a break in my own club, or do you think I should keep letting it slide?" He wasn't sure if the question was rhetorical. The only thing he was aware of was the unfamiliar need to keep the conversation going. "Should I keep rejecting the same women over and over again every time I enter the Vault, even though they already know the score?"

"How do they know the score?" Her voice softened, the bitter edge of spite seeping away.

"I always make it clear I don't sleep with the same woman twice. I never leave any doubt." That hadn't changed since the first night the Vault doors had opened.

"You never made it clear to me."

No, he hadn't. Their position was different. "We haven't slept together yet." *Yet?* His subconscious tacked on the additional word without his approval.

"Well..." She lowered her gaze to his shoes. "I guess addressing the issue wasn't uncalled for. But you could've handled it better. You should've been nice."

"I don't do nice."

Her grin produced a dimple, and soft laughter followed.

"You're laughing at *me* now?" He should've been annoyed. Instead, he found himself grinning back at her. It didn't make a lick of sense. Then again, he rarely had women making fun of him. They were always making plans to fuck him. "I thought we weren't allowed to do that."

"I can't help it. You sound like a five-year-old throwing a tantrum. I can picture you using the same tone to say, 'I don't *do* vegetables.'"

"I *do* do vegetables," he countered. "What I don't do is put up with people's shit. I'm just sorry you got caught in the crossfire."

"Really?" She quirked a disbelieving brow.

"Yeah. Really."

She gave a soft snort and threw her handbag onto the passenger seat. "Thanks for letting me know."

"Does that mean we're good now?"

She nibbled her bottom lip. There was no seduction. Only contemplation. And holy shit, it was worth more on a sexual scale than any lip bite he'd previously witnessed. The sight sent his mind into a rapid rewind to the night in the locker room. Her body resting against his. Her moans filling his ears.

"I suppose so."

His dick started cashing checks his mind wasn't willing to pay. "I'm glad to hear it." He backtracked, getting out of there. Fast. "I'll see you around."

"Nope." She slid into the driver's seat. "I won't be back."

"Then, I guess it was nice knowing you."

She chuckled again and began closing her door. "I wouldn't go that far, either."

CHAPTER SEVEN

A shitty mood didn't come close to what Bryan sported when he shoved past the glass doors of the Taste of Sin restaurant the following day. The scheduled lunch shift wasn't the issue. The problem came from his phone.

He'd expected the sperm vultures to have left a message or two while his cell lay dormant overnight. The snatch pics that filled his text box hadn't been a surprise. He'd also expected the abusive message from Leo over what had happened last night.

What he hadn't predicted was the message from Tera—*If you change your mind and want to talk, please call me.*

Oh, hell, no. He wasn't going to let her fuck up another day. As far as he was concerned, his parents were already dead and buried. He assumed the feeling was mutual.

The reminder to change his cell number had him in a shitty mood. But from the sight of his business partners standing beside a table in the empty dining room of Taste of Sin, the worst was yet to come.

T.J. maintained his usual friendly expression—casual smile, laid-back posture. On the flip side, Leo scowled, eyeing him as if eagerly awaiting the start of whatever intervention was on this week's agenda.

"What are you doing here?" Bryan veered to the left, cutting through the tables toward the storage room behind the bar. "I thought you were both working tonight."

"We are." T.J. cleared his throat and shot a glance at Leo. "We have a few things we wanted to discuss with you beforehand."

"Right..." He continued walking, unsurprised when they both followed into the small enclosed area behind the bar. They hovered inside the doorway as Bryan dumped his wallet and keys in the safe. "Hurry up and get it over with."

"You went too far last night." Leo stepped inside and pulled the door shut behind them. "I had no idea of the extent of what happened until after you bailed. Then all hell broke loose, and I had a mass of women nagging me about how I was going to address the situation."

"Address the situation? You're joking, right? I followed club rules. I did everything by the book. The women in the Vault were due for a reminder on club etiquette, so I made a public announcement." No harm. No foul. At least from his viewpoint. "If you'd been getting snatch pics every five minutes and throaty voice messages the next, you would've done the same damn thing."

"I get it." T.J. gave him a placating look, furrowed brow and all. "Leo said a few of the women were hounding you—"

"A few?" Bryan glared at Leo. "If you're going to relay a story, at least tell it right."

"Okay, so a population equivalent to the Chinese army has been begging to nail you. Better?" Leo rolled his eyes. "You already know my feelings on the matter. You can't deny you overreacted."

Bryan ground his teeth. Had his friends already forgotten what it was like to be single in a club of voracious women? Did they even remember why they'd opened the Vault?

No. Of course not.

They were too busy creating memories with their significant others, and in return, shifting the dynamic of the business. T.J. had reconciled with his wife, Cassie, and Leo and Shay were growing closer with every public display of affection. Decisions surrounding the running of Taste of Sin, Shot of Sin, and the Vault of Sin were no longer a closed discussion.

"I go to the Vault to relax," he grated. "I'm not going to put up with any crap down there. It was created for us. We opened it. We made the rules."

"And now it's a thriving business." T.J. leaned against a stack of beer cartons next to the door. "It's moved beyond an irregular night of fun and is growing into something bigger than any of us planned."

"Then maybe it should go back to the way it was." He didn't believe the words coming out of his mouth. He didn't mean them. But something had to change. He just didn't know what.

His friends frowned, matching expressions of disbelief hitting him with their subtle annoyance.

"You're the one who suggested these show nights," Leo bit out.

Demonstrations. They were demonstrations or classes, not shows, but Bryan kept the critique to himself.

"You wanted to increase satisfaction levels and talk about getting women off efficiently. You were the one who suggested a BDSM talk session in the future. Now, all of a sudden, we're moving too fast? You can't have it both ways."

Bryan ran a hand over his forehead and massaged his temples. "I know."

Tera's phone call had him on edge. To the point of

angered hysteria. After years of continuously burying the memories of his past, one twenty-second conversation had dragged everything to the forefront.

"Come on, man. You know the Vault is holding its own when it comes to income." T.J.'s voice softened. "Membership has doubled. The nights we open are increasing due to demand. And there's a shitload of interest in the class you've organized."

"There *was*," Leo clarified. "I doubt it will go ahead now."

"What?" Bryan dropped his hand to his side. "Why?"

He'd put weeks of work into curating the perfect information session. With the influx of new members, there'd been a slight decline in enjoyment from the female patrons. The intention was to encourage men currently more interested in their own orgasms into those who gained greater pleasure in providing them to others.

"You stirred a hornet's nest last night. After you left, half the members were up in arms, screaming for blood."

"Let me guess," Bryan scoffed. "The female half?"

"Nailed it." Leo glared through tiny slits. "So how are you going to fix this?"

Fix this? He balled his hands into fists, the divide between them increased. There was nothing to fix. Not on his end.

"Like I said, I had women hassling me last night. I reminded them of the rules. End of story." He made for the door. "If they can't take a stern warning, they shouldn't be in the club."

"That's not what they're pissed about. They're saying you singled out a woman in one of the private rooms. They're demanding an apology."

"He's not exaggerating." T.J. pulled his cell from his jacket pocket. "I received a few messages about it this morning. Cassie did, too."

Bryan brushed the offered phone away and grabbed the

door handle. "Well, then, they're in luck, because I already apologized to Ella last night. This shit is dead and buried." He winced when the words reminded him of his mother.

"Did you really apologize?"

Bryan turned to Leo. "Do I look like I give enough fucks to lie about it?" He was many things, but a liar wasn't one of them. His friends knew it, too.

"Good." The concern in T.J.'s features didn't lessen. "That's a start. They're still going to want a public apology, but if we send everyone an email clarifying what happened in the aftermath of the confrontation, maybe the class can go ahead."

"A public apology?" A public fucking apology? Were they kidding? "That's not going to happen."

"Then neither will the class." Leo spread his arms wide. "You can't have one without the other."

"That's how it's going to be?" Fury slithered through his veins, making his fingers shake, his heart palpitate. He took a menacing step toward Leo, trying like hell to keep his emotions in check. "You're railroading me into doing something I shouldn't have to do?"

"Are you really going to get in my face over this?" Leo raised his chin. "What's gotten into you? I warned you yesterday to keep it friendly. Now look what's happened—the women have quit salivating over your bullshit. Even Janeane has a prickle up her snatch and has refused to be your plaything for the demonstration night."

A prickle, otherwise known as rejection revenge. "I don't need her help." God knew he'd been scraping the bottom of the barrel when it came to his enthusiasm over using someone with claws poised to sink into his skin.

"Well, you're going to need someone, and none of the women in the Vault will touch you. They've already vowed to stick together to make a point."

"We're not the only club in town. I'll find someone else."

"That's beside the point. Nobody will show up to the demo as a spectator for the same reason." T.J. slid his cell into his jacket pocket. "You know I love you, man, but this is our reputation you're playing with. You either need to apologize or get the woman back in here to prove everything's been smoothed over."

"I agree," Leo added. "Or maybe think about stepping away from the Vault until it all blows over."

"Step away?"

Fuck.

He got it, really, he did. The women were playing the emotional, we-did-nothing-wrong card, and all the men were standing beside them because otherwise they wouldn't get laid.

Well played, ladies. Well played.

"I can't do that." The Vault was his go-to. His one hangout. His only refuge. He'd never needed the mind-numbing escape more. "Not right now."

"And why is that?" Leo asked. "You haven't been an eager participant for months."

Now they were keeping tabs on him? "Because Shay keeps asking to ride my dick and I'm just about ready to cave."

Leo glared. "Sarcasm? Now there's something new for a change. You could've simply asked me to mind my own business."

"I'm pretty sure I've done that more times than I can count. It looks like Shay is starting to rub off on you."

"Come on, guys." T.J. pushed from the stack of beer cartons. "We need to sort this mess. The demo is next Thursday night, and we don't have another party planned in the Vault beforehand."

There was no *we* involved. This was all on Bryan's

shoulders. Along with all the other shit that had piled on top of him this week.

"Don't worry. I'll work it out." Bryan made for the door, determined to put this bullshit behind him to make way for the more important bullshit.

"Yeah?" Leo followed behind him. "And how do you plan on doing that?"

"It'll be an easy fix." He shrugged. "I'll convince Ella to be my assistant."

CHAPTER EIGHT

*P*amela handed the carry-out coffee and muffin to the construction worker who had become a regular customer in her cafe. He was a nice guy. Always placed a generous tip in her jar. Constantly gave her a sweet grin. Never wavered with his manners. "Enjoy."

He inclined his head, backtracking as he increased the sugary sweetness of his smile. "Thank you. I will."

Her sister, Kim, groaned from her position in front of the coffee machine. "The studs are out in force today. I feel like we've hit the hot-guy jackpot."

"He's not *that* hot." Pamela placed the glass dome back on top of the muffin display plate. "Too cute and sweet for my appetite."

"I'm not talking about Muffin Man. I want to latch my nails into the guy out front. He's been standing there on his cell for five minutes, and I'm dying to know if he's going to come inside."

Pamela swung her gaze to the door and swallowed over the gasp threatening to escape her throat. The man's face was annoyingly familiar—the scowl even more so.

Bryan. The asshole who'd kept her up all night pondering hate sex.

"Shit." She scooted behind Kim, hiding from view. It wasn't the first time she'd seen him walk by her little café, but it was the first time he'd stopped.

"You know him?"

"Technically? No."

"But..."

"That's Bryan—the guy from the club I was telling you about." She clutched her sister's arm, dragging her along the counter like a shield.

"The one with superior hands and an unrivaled bad attitude?"

"Yes. Now get me out of here before he sees me."

They shuffled in unison toward the swinging kitchen doors until she safely hid from view. Now all she had to deal with was the raised questioning brow coming from her mother behind the preparation bench.

"Who are we hiding from?" Her mom craned her neck, paused in her task of peeling carrots as she looked out the service window.

"Nobody." Pamela smiled and crossed her hands behind her back. "I just wanted to see what you're up to."

The raised brow didn't waver.

"You're such a bad liar," Kim whispered.

At this point, Pamela didn't care. She just wanted to remain in hiding, not tempting fate, until Bryan continued down the street.

"I think he's gone." Kim nudged the door open, peeking out the small space. "I can't see him anymore."

Relief, thick and delicious, pulsated in Pamela's chest. "Thank God." She didn't have the energy to deal with assholes today. Not even good-looking ones. But just to be sure, she glanced through the slight part of the doors and scanned the sidewalk.

Nope. Not there.

"Wait." Her sister indicated a man at the counter, his back toward them. "Is that him?"

The guy she pointed to had a similar build—broad shoulders covered in a tailored suit. Only the blond hair was all wrong. Too short. No beard.

"No. That's not him."

"You sure? Isn't he the guy who was out the front?"

"What guy out the front?" Their mom squeezed between them, her voice a conspiratorial whisper.

"Forget it." Pamela stepped back from the door, her cheeks warming. Was she hallucinating now? She could've sworn she'd seen Bryan. Then again, her thoughts had been obsessed with him since he'd broken her non-masturbatory orgasm drought. Not even his nastiness had abated the X-rated daydreams.

"I must've been mistaken." She leaned against the counter beneath the service window and winced. "That guy doesn't look anything like him."

Kim frowned at her, the glance speaking of a shared concern to Pamela's mental stability. "I need to get back out there. We'll discuss this later." She pushed through the doors, disappearing into the main room of the café.

"Did you get enough sleep?" Her mother scrutinized her, the concern in her eyes a familiar sight since Lucas died.

"I slept fine... Or maybe I didn't. I don't know." She shrugged. "I'm at that age where sleep is more of a luxury than a necessity."

The close examination continued. "You had another bad night."

This time it wasn't a question. After Lucas passed away, her mom had become a master at reading all the things

Pamela tried to keep to herself. And years later, the game of hide and seek hadn't ended.

"I went to the club last night. That's all. You know I don't get much sleep when I've been out."

"It seems like more than that to me."

She waggled her brows, hoping to kill the questions with her mother's discomfort. "Maybe I got laid."

"The luggage under your eyes isn't the I-got-laid type. But you know I'm here whenever you're ready to talk." Her mother returned to the preparation bench and picked up a carrot from the chopping board.

Pamela stood there, hard bench behind her, concerned parent in front. She didn't want to talk anymore. There'd been years and years of it. All conversations revolved around Lucas and how she needed to live her life now that he was gone.

Like her time at the Vault, she needed to move on and realize this new chapter wasn't a failure. It was merely going to be different. Devoid of sexual motivation, but not necessarily crummy.

Oh, who was she kidding.

Her sex life had taken a nose-dive and she was still cleaning up after the crash and burn, hoping to salvage something from the charred remains.

"Thanks." She gave her mom a sad smile and pushed from the counter. "I better go and help Kim."

"Ella?"

Holy shit.

Her eyes widened as the masculine voice washed over her, the dominant presence tickling the back of her neck.

Her mother paused, carrot in hand, and glanced through the service window. Pamela didn't need to turn around to determine who owned the deep growl.

Then again, maybe this was another hallucination.

She swung around, coming face to face with Bryan standing on the other side of the window.

"Have you got a minute?" The question came casually. As if they were friends. As if she should've expected him to walk back into her life today.

"Do you know him?" her mother hissed, dragging Pamela's attention back to maternal eyes now twinkling with appreciation for a man who was completely undeserving.

"Unfortunately."

Appreciation turned to excitement. "Come in. Come in." Her mother waved a hand, her matchmaker switch well and truly engaged.

Oh, no.

No, no, no.

"*Mom.*"

The warning was ignored, the kitchen door swung open, and the devil entered, shrinking the room with his presence.

"Morning, ma'am." Bryan smiled at her mother.

Smiled and used the word *ma'am*.

What the hell was he playing at? The contrast from the stuck-up, superior man she knew didn't compute. Not in the slightest. This guy had a casual air of the-boy-next-door, with a smooth swagger and gentle eyes.

"Morning, Ella."

She didn't offer a greeting. Not in words. Her frown posed as a technicolor response.

"Can we talk?"

She worked the question over in her mind. Back and forth. "Didn't we speak last night?"

His lips twitched, a tiny hitch of mirth. "We did. And now I have something else I want to discuss."

"Take a seat in the café," her mother offered unwanted assistance. "I'll help Kim for a while."

Bryan raised a questioning brow to confirm the option.

"No," she growled. "We can speak here."

He sucked in a slow, deep breath, showing his displeasure with a subtle expand of his broad chest. "Sure." His gaze leisurely glided from her to her mother, back and forth. "Are we still good after last night?"

"As good as we're going to get."

There were no grudges. Not really... Okay, she hadn't slept a wink due to her body wanting him and her mind hating him. With time, her annoyance probably would've faded. But less than twenty-four hours had passed, so he was out of luck.

"Hint taken." His tongue worked over the words like he was seducing them. Or her. She feared he succeeded in both. "I have a proposition for you."

She shook her head. "Not interested."

"You don't want to hear me out?"

"I ditched the sucker-for-punishment attitude twelve hours ago."

Another glance went from mother to daughter before his expression changed. It was slight. The minute squint of his eyes, the tiniest tilt of his chin. "This has nothing to do with punishment." He stared at her, stared so hard her betraying nipples tingled. "It's the opposite."

The opposite of punishment?

She shuddered. Her built-up tension and annoyance formed a concoction that resembled arousal. All the while, her mother remained quiet. Still a few feet away. Still mesmerized by a man who deserved far less scrutiny.

"On second thought, let's take this outside." She dragged her feet to the kitchen doors, shoving through them to enter the dining area.

It wasn't safe to be caged in the small kitchen with him. Fresh air became necessary. Space, too. She walked onto the street and took a seat at one of the steel-frame tables that were usually only occupied during the really busy times when customers had nowhere else to sit.

He followed, and the split second when he loomed close, about to take his seat, was a threatening taunt to all her needy senses. She wanted him over her. Under her. Inside her.

Christ.

"What do you want, Bryan?" Her voice cracked with the built-up tension clogging her throat.

He sat opposite her, dwarfing the setting, the metal table and chairs appearing toy-like under his large frame.

The problematic situation only intensified when Kim strode onto the sidewalk, a notepad in hand, and stopped at their table. "May I take your order?"

Pamela scowled. They didn't provide table service. Never had. "No, Kim. We're good."

"I'll get a large coffee, strong, with cream, thanks." Bryan held her focus while he ordered. Asserting his authority. Vocalizing his confidence.

Wrong decision, buddy. He'd flaunted his head-strong independence in the wrong place. Especially when it came to her protective sister.

"Sure thing." Kim scribbled on the notepad. "I'll be back in a second."

Pamela focused farther down the footpath, unwilling to stare into his deep blue eyes. It didn't make sense that she could loathe and lust for a man, all at the same time. She wished one emotion would hurry up and claim victory because this seesaw was exhausting.

"We're not good, are we?" He leaned back in his chair. "Even though you said so last night."

"Last night we were good because I never thought I'd see you again."

His mouth tilted as if she'd paid him a compliment. Sharp

eyes turned gentle. Harsh lips became inviting. "What if I decided I'm not finished with you yet?"

She laughed, a cold, bitter laugh she hoped sounded convincing. It wasn't the first time he'd said 'yet' and had it sound like a sexual promise. Both instances had been equally confusing. "Then I'd take pleasure in letting you down gently. Just like you did to me last night."

"I see you like to hold a grudge."

"Only as much as most women."

He gave a breath of a chuckle, the sound lacking humor. She waited, hoping to see a believable smile pulling at that lush mouth.

Nothing came.

Nothing but her sister who slid a take-away coffee in front of him with a slight curtsy. "Here you go, Bryan. Enjoy."

"Thanks." He focused on the container as Kim walked away, his hand snaking up to rub over his beard. "She knows my name?"

"She knows a lot of things." There were no skeletons left hidden to her family. No rock left unturned. Pamela rarely had anything to be ashamed of, and even when she did, telling her sister seemed like a form of penance.

"So, it's likely she spat in my coffee."

"No, it's not likely." She spoke with solemn sincerity, allowing him the time to relax and reach for his take-away cup before she added, "It's a certainty. There is no way in hell that coffee doesn't contain some sort of retribution."

His smile turned to a grin. When laughter hit her ears, she sat back and stared. Carefree Bryan was remarkable. A picture of charming severity. The playfulness in his eyes swept away his hostility, those flawless white teeth no longer vicious.

He placed the cup down as his happiness dissipated and the man she knew returned, this time less harsh.

"Are you ready to tell me why you're here?"

He raised his gaze to her, those blue eyes lingering on her lips longer than necessary. "After we left last night, some of the Vault members announced their annoyance at how I spoke to you. In fact, a lot of the women are up in arms, demanding a public apology."

"Public apology?" She glanced around, hoping he had no intention of making a scene in front of her café.

"Don't worry, I already told my business partners I've done the necessary groveling. I don't plan on doing it again."

She rolled her eyes. "Why am I not surprised?"

"I'm hoping it's because you realize we've already resolved the situation and dragging it out would be bullshit."

"Okay." She shrugged. "But you still haven't answered my question. Why are you here?"

"Did you get the email I sent about the class I'm running next Thursday night? A guys' tutorial on the female—"

"Yeah. I got it."

"Then, you'll also know I plan on having a demonstration assistant."

She remembered. Her imagination had run wild with the thought of watching the instructional performance. "And?"

"And Janeane, the woman who was supposed to play the role, is one of the people demanding an apology. I need someone to take her place."

"That shouldn't be difficult. Not with women scrambling to climb on your junk."

He nodded, as if pondering his immense self-worth. "Finding a willing woman wouldn't be too hard. I'm more concerned with finding the right one. That's why I'm here."

She laughed. He had to be joking. There was no way in hell a man could have balls big enough to ask that of her after the way he'd treated her. "You want *me* to be your assistant?"

"Yes." The answer came strong and sure. No doubt. No guilt.

Another laugh escaped. "Are you kidding?"

The tight set of his jaw implied he wasn't.

"Is this some sort of game? You thought I was interested in you, so you shot me down in flames, and now that you realize I have no intention in joining your drama-llama lifestyle you decide you want my help?" She pushed back in her chair, ready and oh, so willing to bail.

"I came here because you're the perfect fit for this demonstration—"

"Out of all the women at the Vault, *I'm* the perfect fit?"

"There's no one else." His nostrils flared and he stilled, taking precious moments before he said, "What happened last night has ensured nobody else will help me. Not without the public apology I refuse to give."

"Oh." She batted her lashes, the picture of sweet innocence. "I get it now. You *need* me," she enunciated the words, letting them dance over her tongue. "Isn't this a delicious curve ball?"

"I don't need you, Ella. I can cancel the class. It's no skin off my nose. But working together would benefit us both."

"No." She pushed back in her chair, preparing to stand. "It wouldn't benefit me at all."

"Are you sure about that?" His tone dropped, having a torturous effect on her belly. "You came to the Vault in search of something. And you know I can give it to you."

"You *could*," she corrected. "Back when you hadn't grated every one of my nerves. For me, mental stimulation is ten times more effective than physical. There's no way you could get me to cross the line now I have a clearer picture of who you are."

"Don't assume to know me." He held her captive with his fierce stare. "We've spent little more than an hour together."

An hour that packed the punch of a three-year obsession.

"Look..." She sighed. "Maybe if last night hadn't happened, I'd consider it. But I didn't exaggerate what I told you in the parking lot."

She wasn't interested. She couldn't be.

He raised a brow. "Not even about the livestock?"

She snorted over his unexpected humor. "Okay, so maybe I exaggerated about the livestock. But that's all. You're not my type and I'm definitely not looking for complications." She'd had enough to last a lifetime. "Enjoy your coffee. I need to get back to work."

She pushed from her seat and stepped away, only to be stopped by a large hand clasping her wrist, the fingers delicate in their hold.

He glanced up at her. "I don't need to be your type to get you off."

He was right. So damn right her uterus squeezed, begging her to concede. Every part of her reacted to him in an unforgiving way. Her skin buzzed. Her heart fluttered. The nerves he'd grated to stubs were waving wildly with energetic excitement.

"Yeah, you do." She knew her sexual limits, even if her body wasn't predictable at the moment.

"So, your rapid pulse is from what?" He tilted his head. "And the goose bumps?" He trailed his thumb along the inside of her wrist. Teasing. Tormenting. "You may not like me. But you're still attracted to me."

He released his hold and stood. All male. All muscle. "What happened the night in the locker room is a drip in the ocean to what I have planned for the class."

A drip?

She kept her chin high, even though her breasts ached. All she could do was shake her head, no longer able to voice a rejection.

"I've proven you wrong once before. Give me the chance to do it again."

"While under the scrutiny of a crowd at the club? No, thanks." She walked for the café doors, even though her libido remained begging at his feet. Her interest was temporary. A sleep-deprived delusion. There was no doubt he'd be unsuccessful a second time around.

Okay, maybe there was a little doubt.

A teeny, tiny bit.

Not enough to justify further humiliation, though.

"What if we had a test run?"

His question pulled her up short. She turned, finding him clutching the backrest of his metal chair.

"A test run?"

"I can open the Vault tonight. For the two of us. That way we can see who's right or wrong."

"I know my body." At least she had, until Bryan had scorched her with his touch.

"I remember you thinking the same thing in the locker room."

She scoffed, wishing she had a smart quip to shove in his face. Unfortunately, they both knew he was right. He'd tweaked parts of her she'd thought died years ago.

"You like to keep throwing that in my face, don't you?"

"If it helps me get what I want." He shrugged. "I'll do whatever's necessary."

Her chest squeezed with the close proximity to defeat. "I'm not going to the club. If you want to do this, we do it my way." The response felt like surrender. Tantalizing, erotic surrender.

"I'm listening."

She approached, taking one cautious step after another. The ball rested in her court; all she needed to do was determine what she wanted to gain.

His discomfort.

The tiniest taste of retribution.

"You need to meet me at my apartment." Where he'd be surrounded by her things and would no doubt feel uncomfortable in a scary, relationship-type setting. If they were going to do this, he needed to hate every single minute of it.

He didn't flinch. "Your place, it is. Would you also like to dictate the time?"

"Seven." The power trip was invigorating. "I'll get a piece of paper to write down the address."

"Don't worry about it. I have all your details at the club."

So, that was how he'd found her.

He released the back of the chair and straightened to his full domineering height. "I'll see you tonight, Ella, and I'll bring dinner."

Dinner? Like a date?

He pulled a wallet from his back pocket and retrieved a ten-dollar bill. "For the coffee."

"I don't want your money." She didn't even want his conversation. All she was willing to gain from her time with him was orgasms.

"Thanks." He encroached, putting her on edge. His aftershave danced around her, the slightest scent of sexuality teasing her senses. "I guess I'll pay you back tonight."

She wouldn't shudder. She refused. "We'll see."

"Yeah." His eyes danced, devilish, predatory, and so damn cocky. "We will."

CHAPTER NINE

*B*ryan reached her doorstep five minutes early, bottle of wine under one arm, bags of Chinese take-out in the other. He'd made the right assumption about her wealth. She lived in an expensive suburb, her complex surrounded by manicured gardens and an impressive security system.

It got him thinking about where she got the money. It was either Daddy's or the dead husband's. You didn't get digs like this on a barista's paycheck.

He knocked on her door with a gentle knuckle, knowing she'd already be waiting after having to buzz him into the building.

Seconds later, the door opened and Ella stood before him, one hand clutching the handle as she rocked a loose grey shirt and a pair of cotton, sporty short-shorts.

"You found the place easy enough?"

"No problem at all."

He hadn't expected this—her no-fucks-given attire, the lack of seduction. She dressed simple. Carefree. There was no hint of her trying to impress him, and funnily enough, she had anyway. He couldn't even smell perfume. Only the faint hint of citrus soap mingling with the Asian spices wafting from their dinner.

"Something wrong?" She frowned, her questioning eyes reading him.

"I'm surprised, that's all. I didn't know what to expect when I arrived."

"You thought you'd get lingerie and scented candles?" She nailed it with a smile. A cute, light-hearted lift of sweet lips. "Let me remind you, you're not the stud you think you are. I get that you're the king of orgasms in the Vault. But out here, in the real world, you're kind of a dick."

"So you keep telling me." He held up the bags containing their dinner. "You going to let me in before this gets cold?"

"Oh, sorry." She stepped back, sweeping her hand to the apartment behind her as if he were royalty. "I guess I was expecting you to pound your chest and demand entry."

"Very funny."

"I thought so."

Her apartment was pristine. Nothing out of place. Pillows lined her brown leather sofa. Magazines were neatly stacked on the coffee table. The carpet had fresh vacuum marks, the furniture was polished. She had her shit together, at least better than he did.

"Where do you want to eat?"

"Dinner table."

He continued ahead to the open dining and kitchen area, placing the food and wine on the large wooden setting.

Ella busied herself riffling through cupboards and drawers, then came to stand beside him with plates and cutlery. "Do you think you ordered enough?" Her sarcasm was rich as she helped him place the containers in the middle of the table.

Truth was, he hadn't known what she'd like. He didn't even know if she enjoyed Chinese food, so he'd ordered a variety to satisfy every palate. "You can't order Chinese without leaving enough for leftovers. They're the best part."

She nodded, buying his bullshit. "What would you like to drink? I don't have beer, but I have some of Lucas's scotch and bourbon hidden in the kitchen somewhere."

"I'm happy to share the wine with you."

She eyed him skeptically. "Sure."

"Something wrong?" he mocked, taking on the same tone she'd used earlier.

"Yeah. You're being nice."

"How?"

"The wine. The mass of Chinese food. What gives?"

She was right. This moment escaped his typical normality, but he wasn't willing to admit how badly he needed her to smooth things over at the Vault.

"Sweetheart, there's nothing nice about it. I'm starving, and I need as much alcohol to get through this as you do."

"And there he is, the Brute I've come to know and despise." She slid into her seat across the table, dragging a plate and cutlery in front of her. "But you know what? I think you're making excuses, because deep down you think I'm super-dooper awesome." She waggled her perfectly manicured brows.

He couldn't tell if her pretty smile was annoying, or way too endearing. Either way, it had an effect on his chest he wasn't used to. And he was surprised her laugh didn't make him want to shudder. "You're not too bad."

She chuckled and dished food onto her plate while he poured the wine. They didn't talk for long moments. Strangely enough, they didn't need to. He had no desire to fill the silence. And going by the pleased look on her face, she had no problem with the absence of conversation, either.

While they ate, he took the time to read her. Finding out tiny snippets of her character with the visual sweep. She chewed slowly. Unrushed bites with dazed contemplation. She didn't gulp at her wine as if consumed with nervousness. She didn't fidget or fiddle. Despite having a low tolerance to his attitude, she seemed to feel comfortable with him.

"Have you lived here long?" He had a sudden urge to learn more. To dig deeper.

"About a year."

"And you've been a widow for how long?"

Her fork slipped, missing food and splashing sauce onto the table. She stared at the dark brown droplet now marring the wood and frowned. "Long enough."

The vibrancy of her eyes turned bleak. Her smile faded, and in its place, sorrow grew. She cleared her throat and ran a lazy finger over the dribble, bringing the liquid to her lips to lick away the mess. For a second, he became mesmerized by her far-off contemplation. She was emotionally bare, her pain almost tangible.

He shouldn't push, and not merely due to manners. He didn't want to give her the wrong impression and make her think he gave a shit. But he needed answers, for no other reason than to understand who this woman was.

"How long were you married?"

She reached for her wine, dragging out the seconds as she took a long gulp. "Eleven months."

"You must've been young." He was fishing for answers because he hadn't had time to re-read the finer details of her file when he snooped for her café address.

She barked out a laugh. "How old do you think I am?"

Good question. *Tricky* question.

He scrutinized her—the young eyes, the ruby lips. She didn't have a wrinkle in sight, yet she grasped her sexuality like a woman far older than her appearance suggested.

"Late twenties?"

Her mouth quirked and he had the sudden urge to kiss

her. There was no romance about it. He wasn't interested in a chaste kiss. What he pictured was something harsh and unforgiving. Something dirty to wash away the tainted widow.

"You just earned yourself a gold star." She placed her fork on her plate and inched them both toward the middle of the table.

"I'm right?"

"No. But I'll take it as a compliment." She pushed to her feet. "Do you want seconds, or should I put the containers in the fridge?"

"I'm good." Too good.

He enjoyed knowing they were closer in age than he'd previously assumed. But again, the added information only increased the need for more. He wanted to know everything. Was she still hung up on the love of a dead man? How had she found his sex club? And how did she plan to sate her sexuality if she didn't return to the Vault?

He shoved the last piece of honey chicken into his mouth as she stacked containers back into the bag. Her loose top gaped at the front, the fucking brilliant view of her bra-covered tits staring him right in the face.

From any other woman, he would've considered the act a blatant attempt at seduction. From Ella, he didn't get that vibe at all. She was oblivious to her temptation and confident enough in her own right not to be embarrassed about a glimpse of intimate skin. It was clear she also had no clue of the filthy thoughts rapidly building in his mind—the need to prove her wrong, to make her fully aware of the control he could gain over her body. He wanted to have her pussy clamping around his fingers. Her thighs clenching around his head. Her lips parting to call his name, louder than she'd ever called before.

Because that was what he was good at.

The only thing he was good at.

He snatched the wine bottle from beside her and filled their glasses. The comfortable silence had turned chaotic. A hint of panic tinged the air, or maybe it only lingered in his blood.

"How many times have you done this?" He needed to know where he ranked on the list. What was his number in the line?

"Had wine and Chinese food?" She didn't meet his gaze as she lifted the bag and made for the kitchen.

"Brought someone from the club back to your apartment?"

She shrugged. "This is the first time I've had any man in my apartment."

"The first?" He followed, dirty dish and full wine glass in hand. "I thought Shay said you'd been a widow for years."

"And now you're taking the invitation as a compliment?" She opened the fridge, shooting him an unimpressed glance over the top of the door as she placed the food inside. "Don't. Believe me, you're not special. I just haven't had much luck with men since Lucas passed."

With every insult, he struggled to hide his smirk. Her compounding disinterest had the opposite effect on him. A dangerous effect. For once, he felt a strange pull for more.

"Maybe that will change after the demonstration night."

She closed the fridge and came toward him, taking the plate from his hands to place it in the sink. "You've gotta get me there first, bucko."

"I guess you're ready for me to prove my worth. Tell me where you want to do this and we'll get started."

"Now?" She turned from the sink, her eyes wide. "God, no. I just ate a truckload of food. Unless you have a pregnancy fetish, you're going to have to wait until my belly settles."

No, no pregnancy fetish, but he was starting to think he had a thing for kitchens.

He could picture her bent over the sink. Slammed up against the fridge. Splayed on the counter. He didn't want to wait. He had to get this over and done with before his needs became demands.

"Can we sit for a while?" She made for the dining table to claim her wine glass, bringing a waft of heavenly scented citrus air as she scooted past. "I've been on my feet all day."

He huffed. He didn't even try to hide it.

Her responding chuckle only increased his annoyance.

"Is it going to threaten your bachelor status if we sit side by side on the sofa?"

"Doesn't worry me in the slightest."

"Liar." Her mouth curved in a knowing smile, the wine glass raising to those tempting lips. "I knew being here would make you uncomfortable."

"We'll see who's uncomfortable once you're naked and writhing. I figure the apology you're going to owe me for doubting my skills will be hard to spit out."

"I'm never going to apologize for not being endeared by your shitty attitude." She strode into the living room, an added sway to those hips. "If you can work any sort of magic it will merely be a payoff for the crap you've put me through."

His gaze strayed to her ass encased in those tiny sports shorts. If anyone was going through crap, it was him. He was the one who had to figure out how to get her off while holding his own lust in check. Lust that rapidly morphed into a driving force.

He followed her, choosing to stand by the stacked bookshelf while she lazily slumped onto the three-seater sofa. She kicked her feet onto the coffee table, spreading long, smooth legs before him like an appetizer.

"So..." He turned to the bookshelf, taking in the middle

shelf stacked wall to wall with cancer information. A cold ache formed under his sternum at the thought of the nightmare his parents were enduring. He wanted to familiarize himself with their suffering, to pretend he was involved somehow. "That's a lot of books."

There were emotional titles—*When Breath Becomes Air*, *Everyday Strength*, and *How to Help Someone with Cancer*. Research titles—*Radical Remission*, *What You Need to Know About Cancer*, *The Facts 101*. Even those that promoted alternate therapies.

"Lucas had terminal cancer."

He'd guessed as much. "I'm sorry you had to go through that."

"Don't be. It's not your fault."

He pulled a title from the shelf and stared at the couple on the cover—*Supporting Someone with Cancer: A Loved One's Guide*.

He wondered if his father had this book filed neatly on their perfect shelf back in Tampa. Had he purchased all these titles for the woman who made his life worthwhile?

"How much time did you have with your husband after his diagnosis?"

"Eleven months."

He frowned and shoved the book back into place. "I thought you said you were married for eleven months."

"I did." She sipped from her glass, her eyes trained on his. "It's a long story."

"Do you mind if I ask what it's like?"

"Cancer?" Her forehead wrinkled.

"Yeah. What's the process? The end game?"

Her mouth opened and closed. Her eyes remained wide.

"Sorry, is that a shitty question?"

She snorted through a sip of wine, then placed the glass

down on the coffee table. "I guess it depends why you're asking."

He could've given a lame excuse. He could've lied. "My mother has terminal cancer."

"Oh, Bryan. I'm so sorry." Her face scrunched with genuine sympathy, masking all her beauty and replacing it with pathetic emotion.

"Don't be." He stepped over her legs and took a seat beside her. "We're not close."

"But still, she's your mother. The news must be devastating."

The fact his mother had withheld the information from her only son was more traumatic.

"Feel free to take any of the books home with you. They're no use to me anymore."

"No. I'm good." He could ask a question or two to feel connected to a family who disowned him, but he refused to spend hours researching his mother's downfall. He never should've mentioned her in the first place.

"Well, I'll leave the offer open if you change your mind." Her voice turned somber, her expression, too. "I've been meaning to get rid of them for years. Having the reminder stare me in the face every day is getting a little old."

"Thanks." He concentrated on her fingers, noticing how they dug deeper and deeper into the sole of her foot, as if trying to massage the pain away.

"Do you want to talk about it?" She flashed him a look, one that told him she'd battle through this painful conversation, if only for his benefit.

"No." He shook his head. "Not at all."

"Okay. I get it." She flexed her feet, feigning relaxation. "So, tell me, why a class?" The pain didn't leave her features as she blatantly changed the subject. "What will you get out of it?"

"Satisfaction." At least that's what he'd told himself in the planning stages. He'd wanted to tweak the club on the most intimate level. To mold the greedy Vault patrons into more selfless participants.

But that aim didn't hold his interest anymore. Now, the only thing he wanted from the demonstration night was a one-way ticket between Ella's thighs. To sink under her skin, the same way she was crawling under his.

"I don't buy it."

"I don't need you to."

"That's exactly my point. You don't seem the type to willingly help others for the sake of it. And you already have a posse who think you're the messiah of the female orgasm."

"You've got me pegged. After what? Two conversations?"

Her lips curved, the grief gradually seeping away. "Don't you think I deserve to know, considering I'm contemplating helping you?"

"Helping me? We both know this is mutually beneficial." He jerked his chin toward her feet and indicated for her to lift them in his direction with a crook of his hand.

She frowned, remaining immobile.

He slapped his lap, trying not to make a big deal out of the offer. He wouldn't be able to stop fixating on his parents until she stopped thinking about her husband. And neither thought process was conducive for what he had planned. "Put your feet up here."

Her lips worked over silent contemplation until finally she turned on the sofa, placing her heels on his thighs. "Your fixation on this being mutually beneficial is a load of bull. It's not like I can't get an orgasm without you. I can do the work myself."

"And you're satisfied with that? You don't need a guy to break the monotony?" No matter how she responded, he knew the truth. A woman with her sexuality and passion could never be entirely satisfied with masturbation. It might dull the ache, but she needed to be fucked. There was no substitute for skin on skin.

"I have toys."

He didn't appreciate the visual. Actually, his body appreciated it too damn much. His cock stirred, the hard length nudging against her heel. "I'd like to see that."

"I know," she drawled. "And you wouldn't be the only one."

No doubt. He could sell tickets at the Vault and pack the room with willing voyeurs. She'd enjoy it, too. This woman would love to be the center of innumerable fantasies. She deserved to be.

He grabbed one of her feet, distracting himself as he worked his thumb along her inner sole.

"Oh, God." She groaned. "That feels good."

Shit.

As far as distractions went, this one was counterproductive. Her throaty moans and the arching of her back made his cock push harder against his zipper. And those toenails. Jesus. He'd never spent much time admiring a woman's feet. It wasn't his kink. But he understood it now.

Those dainty, delicate toes.

The feminine light pink polish.

He was in fucking trouble.

How many men came home to this every day? A beautiful woman. A nice meal. Light-hearted conversation. And the promise of a sweaty, energetic fuck.

"I don't get you, Bryan."

Not surprising. He didn't understand himself. Maybe they could work out his insanity together. "What's not to get?"

"You bought me dinner and wine. You're being kind. Well, way beyond civil, anyway. And now you're massaging my feet."

His skin itched with the influx of reality. He'd stopped pretending this woman annoyed him sometime in the last hour. Probably earlier. This afternoon could've been the culprit.

He shrugged it off, determined to snap back on track. "You're not a vulture. It gives me the freedom to relax."

"So, this is the real Bryan?" She scrutinized him, her brows pulled tight. "Far from the brute who torments everyone?"

"I don't torment anyone. Neither do I pretend to be someone I'm not." Not really. He lowered his focus to her feet, gently curling her toes under. "This is me. And the guy you met at the Vault is, too."

She remained quiet, and he didn't dare look at her to fill the void.

"I'm not an asshole, Ella. Not entirely. I just have a low tolerance for bullshit."

She tilted her head, pondering, and he knew exactly what skittered through her mind. He knew it even before she opened her mouth. "Why El—"

"Are you ready to get started?" He tapped her ankles, indicating for her to move. He liked her, but not enough to field questions about his reluctance to say her name.

"Ahh. Sure." She placed her feet on the floor and sat up straight. "How do you want to do this?"

"Let's start with where."

"The bedroom?" Her face remained impassive. "Just in case I get bored and want to take a nap." Her lips twitched, breaking the tension building in his chest.

"The bedroom, it is." He stood, offering her a hand. "And don't worry—you won't be nodding off any time soon."

CHAPTER TEN

The back of Pamela's neck tingled as she led Bryan down the hall. Nervousness had set in, the shaky, uncomfortable feeling an unwanted blast from the past.

"Is something wrong?"

"No, why?" She stopped before her open bedroom door and faced him.

"You were walking like I had a gun at your back."

Why did he care? Before today, she would've assumed it was to exploit her discomfort. But from the way he'd acted tonight, she wondered if the question came from true concern.

"There's a lot of pressure on my shoulders." She hadn't been anxious about sex in a damn long time. Not that this was anxiety as much as it was nervous anticipation.

"There's no pressure." He led the way into her room, not bothering to turn on the light. "All you have to do is relax and let me work my magic. Once I'm done, you can sing my praises, and then I'll leave. Simple as that."

She wasn't going to encourage his confidence. Nope. Not at all.

"I see you hiding a smile under those tight lips." He smirked over his shoulder. "We both know I'm right."

She ignored him and padded to her nightstand to flick on the lamp. The dim light only endeavored to highlight the devilish appeal of his features. His expression spoke of passion. Pleasure and dominance. Everything she'd been searching for since Lucas died stared her in the face, waiting to be grasped in both hands.

If he demanded things of her, things she wasn't necessarily prepared to give, she'd succumb anyway. No doubt. Something inside her had become starved for his approval. She wanted to make him smile again. To ease the sterility that coiled around him with suffocating efficiency.

He inched closer to the bed, his suit pants brushing against the mattress. "Take off your shirt."

Her lips parted in shock, but they shouldn't have. Pleasantries weren't a part of the deal. Neither was foreplay.

She grasped the thin material of her shirt, pulled it over her head, and dropped it to the floor. She stood before him, black lace bra and old cotton shorts. Her chest expanded with the need for more. More air. More control. More noise to fill the tense silence. "Better?"

"Not quite. But we're getting there." His scrutiny raked her. It wasn't a light caress of his attention. It was brutal, like his nickname demanded. Those eyes turned molten, the heat of promise burning bright. "Shorts off, too."

"Wait." Her nervousness came out of hiding, nudging anticipation out of the way. "Should we discuss a rough timeframe to end this?"

He frowned.

"I mean..." She sighed. "If this doesn't seem to be working, should we have a set time in mind to stop? Unlike you, I don't like hurting people's feelings, but I also don't want you all up in my bits, working long hours like a miner, when you're getting nowhere. So, maybe we need a deadline."

He lowered his gaze, paying too much attention to the rapid rise and fall of her chest. "Sure. If it'll make you comfortable, we'll put a fifteen-minute timeline on this."

"Fifteen minutes?" Was he kidding? "I won't even be turned on in fifteen minutes."

He smirked, that wicked lift of lips telling her he already knew she was simmering. "Trust me." He tapped the mattress, encouraging her approach. "I've got this covered."

Her heart kicked.

Parts lower, too.

"Not only will fifteen minutes be enough," he drawled, "but I'm willing to wager I'll get you over the line in less than ten."

"Now you're delusional." She crossed her arms over her chest. "If you're not going to take this seriously—"

"Who's really the delusional one here?" He approached, his sure stride eating up the distance in less than a heartbeat. "The woman who says no man can make her climax?" His hand raised, gently gliding stray strands of hair from her cheek. "Or the guy who achieved it with one finger?"

Her cheeks heated. "Stop bringing that up."

"Why? It was some of my best work."

Some? Whisper-thin threads of jealousy came to life in her chest. She shouldn't have forgotten his efficiency was equally brag-worthy with other women. It was pathetic to even care.

"Are we doing this or what?" She shoved at her shorts, letting them fall to her feet, then climbed onto the bed. "Hurry up. The clock is ticking."

"Not yet, it isn't. We still have the finer details to sort out." He grabbed her ankle and tugged, dragging her toward him. "I've got a ten-minute deadline in this wager. All you need to do is tell me what you want to bet."

She scowled, trying to determine how to dent his arrogance. Their egos were on entirely different playing fields. He was in the pros. She was warming the bench in adolescent D-grade. "If you lose, you spend the night."

No denting occurred. His expression didn't falter.

"In my bed," she continued, hoping to inspire panic. "Like a man who doesn't have a million commitment issues."

The anticipated revulsion didn't reach his features. She hadn't even laid a finger on his bravado.

"Deal."

Was he kidding? Where the hell did his confidence come from?

"And if I win," he purred, "you need to admit, in graphic detail, how my prowess is unlike any other."

"I didn't think you were the type for accolades."

"For you, I'll make an exception." He tugged her closer and let her legs fall over the edge of the mattress.

She clenched her teeth, hating how he'd already made her wet. Her body didn't comply at all. The men she'd wanted to succumb to had no effect, and the one man she didn't want anything to do with was like a sexual healer. Her very own Marvin Gaye. Or was she Marvin in this situation?

Shit.

She couldn't think through the lust fog.

"Any other rules before I start?"

"Yes. I don't kiss on the mouth." She'd had the same stipulation since Lucas died. She didn't want that connection from someone able to walk out the door without a backward glance. The next man she kissed would care for her. He'd cherish the ground she walked on.

"No problem." He splayed a hand over her upper thigh,

his thumb pressing temptingly close to her pussy. "Only touch."

"Good." Her voice croaked.

"Anything else?"

She shook her head.

"Anal? Oral? Foreign objects?" He raised a brow. "Pain? Submission?"

"Now you're just teasing," she murmured. "I'd be surprised if you had time for even one of those in the ten minutes you've allocated."

He snickered, the sound sinister. "Maybe that can be a wager for another day."

Strong fingers gripped the waistband of her panties and tugged. With bold finesse, he exposed the trim strip of curls above her entirely bare pussy and dropped the material to the floor. For long seconds, he stared at her. At *that* part of her, his nostrils flaring, his jaw ticking.

This could be where she gained the upper hand.

She inched back, lying down against the covers, and slowly spread her thighs.

His visual admiration turned to humor, his lips lifting as if he knew her game.

Damn it. How was he so good at this?

"It looks like it's time to start." He glanced at her bedside clock. "It's eight fifty-three."

"Eight fifty-three." She swallowed over the desire clogging her throat.

She was wound tight, eagerly wondering how he planned to win this battle in ten minutes. And if he didn't, how would he deal with a night in her bed? Hell, how the heck would she handle it?

He slid his palm along her leg, toward the apex of her thighs. He held her gaze as the heat of his touch came closer.

A finger, or maybe it was a thumb, skirted gently over the edge of her pussy lips. Delicate and oh, so light. It could barely be considered a touch. It was a breath. A whisper of sensation through the slickness of her arousal.

"I'm surprised you're this wet. Seeing how you're not interested and all." His touched gained pressure, parting her, tempting her opening.

She wanted more. Needed more. "I never said I wasn't interested."

"Right..." Back and forth, his touch raked over her slit, teasing and torturous. "You just lacked faith in my ability."

She opened her mouth, poised to respond when two fingers slid deep, penetrating her, making her back arch off the bed. He curled those digits inside her, finding her sensitive spot faster than she ever found it herself.

No fair.

She clamped her thighs together, tight, and rocked into the rhythmic stroke against her G-spot.

"Still think I can't get you there in another eight minutes?"

"Goddammit. Shut the hell up."

He chuckled, and she didn't understand how he could be unaffected. Maybe that was the reason he kept rejecting women in the Vault. Did he have erection issues?

She lowered her gaze, down his pristine, white dress shirt, to his waistband, then his crotch.

Nope. His reluctance definitely wasn't an arousal issue. The hard, thick length of him strained against his zipper.

He wanted her.

Or maybe he just wanted sex.

Either way, it didn't matter. The thought of his desire made her squirm. Made her throb. Pressure landed on her clit, the spark of enthusiastic tingles taking over her core. He was succeeding. Winning. Not that she wanted him to fail. She craved another of his masterful orgasms.

"You're gorgeous."

The solemn compliment fractured her bliss and she blinked away the confusion to find him visually worshiping her body. The glide of his attention raked her skin, causing havoc, inspiring hysteria.

"The worst part about this agreement is the inability to fuck you." His free hand splayed across her stomach, creeping higher.

"What? Why not?"

"That's not part of the deal." He grasped her covered breast, working the cup down to brush his fingers over her nipple. Back and forth. Up and down.

"Forget the deal," she panted, arching into his touch.

"I wouldn't have time." He grinned, but this curve of lips was half-hearted. "There's only six minutes left."

She whimpered and he responded to her unspoken plea by adding another finger to her pussy. He stretched her, the muscles of her core protesting with a delicious twinge.

"I want your feet on the bed. Soles on the mattress."

She complied, lifting her legs, bending her knees, willing to do anything to continue the bliss.

"Ass up. I want to see you."

Her cheeks warmed as she obeyed, raising her butt off the bed to give him a better view.

"*Fuck*." It was barely a word, his voice more of an incoherent growl. "Tell me what you're thinking. I want to hear those dirty thoughts."

She shook her head, speechless at the ferocity in his eyes. She couldn't think past his touch, the wicked stroke of her G-spot, and the palm massaging her breast. She kept her ass off the bed, each second making her climb higher in search of more.

"Tell me." He glanced at the clock, unhurried as he massaged and coaxed.

They had to be running out of time, but he didn't rush. There was no frantic pace, only a slow build to the perfect rhythm.

"Fucking tell me, Ella, or I stop." His movements slowed, inspiring panic.

"No, don't." Her voice broke. "I want this," she admitted. "I want you."

"*How?*" he snapped.

She continued to shake her head. If she pictured the ways in which she needed him—visualized the two of them together—she'd come. And she wanted that... But she didn't want it, too.

Not yet.

He growled and shoved another finger inside her, her pussy now stretched around four digits. He worked her hard, making her legs burn, her body sweat. He slid his other hand from her breast, over her collarbone, this time stopping at her throat. He held her there, pushing her toward mindlessness with the tight grasp of dominance.

She was close. Her orgasm within a flick of those fingers.

Then he paused.

Fucking stopped.

For seconds or minutes, she didn't know.

"If you don't tell me your dirty thoughts, I don't make you feel good." He appeared to lack concern over the approaching deadline, even though his chest heaved and his eyes blazed. "So, keep talking, sweetheart, or this ends."

"Oh, God," she pleaded, the tingle of bliss fading. She couldn't let it go. Refused. "I never want you to stop touching me. I want to feel you everywhere," she rambled. "I want you to fuck me. And I want it to be hard. So hard it hurts." She wasn't a masochist. Slaps and pinches weren't her thing. The excitement revolved around harsh penetration and vicious thrusts. The thrill of helplessness in the arms of a strong man. "You'd fuck my pussy... My mouth."

His nostrils flared as he groaned. Slowly, the grasp around her throat tightened, increasing her heartbeat. Then the fingers in her cunt twitched. Both sensations were profound on their own. Together they were an exquisite surge of sensation.

She bucked, demanding more. "Then you'd fuck my ass."

The pulse inside her quickened. The squeeze at her throat tightened. His focus held more intent than she'd ever received from him before. Frustration and delirious lust built in those eyes—over her.

He wanted to be inside her, just as much as she needed him there.

She grinned with the knowledge. The pleasure doubled. Multiplied. His fingers kept pace. She whimpered, the sound turning into a mewl. A scream. She tensed, every inch of her becoming a slave to the first pulse of orgasm bursting forward, making her buck.

He didn't stop as she spasmed, calling his name, arching her back. Over and over, he continued to work her, until the pulses lessened. Even then, he didn't stop. In fact, he did the opposite, pressing harder on her clit, spreading her pussy wider.

Another wave hit, blindsiding in its attack.

This orgasm was short but more surprising. The pleasure a breath-taking hit before an equally shocking vacuum. She was capable of multiples now?

She panted through the delirium and slumped against the mattress. When he released her throat, she fought not to show her disappointment. That hold had been transforming. A grasp of nirvana. And those fingers. *Damn him*. They still gently stroked inside her, not letting the bliss entirely fade while his other palm trailed along her sternum, her stomach.

Too much talent had been given to this man. Too much god-like finesse for someone entirely undeserving.

As if reading her mind, his lips quirked. "Are you ready to apologize for doubting my skills, Ella?"

CHAPTER ELEVEN

*H*e'd thrown the bet.

He'd deliberately thrown the whole fucking thing.

She didn't even know yet. She just lay there, blinking up at him with sated, euphoria-glazed eyes.

He hadn't been able to talk himself out of it. She'd been at the mercy of his touch, her perfect body writhing and contorting with each of his movements. Then he'd paused, unable to stand the thought of her coming so soon.

He'd known how much time he'd had left. He'd known exactly how long it would take to get her back to the peak, too, and he'd stopped anyway.

For what? A handful of seconds of her at his mercy?

He couldn't remember a woman ever ensnaring him with erotic fascination. She wasn't merely sexual, she was sensual. A combination of vulnerability and confidence. Carnality and trepidation.

Obviously, he suffered from a case of temporary amnesia. He'd played a hand in innumerable sexcapades. His sexual bucket list had been ticked off long ago. But this was different somehow. If only he could pinpoint the why of it all.

The lust-filled decision to throw the bet was a mistake. And now he was staring down the barrel of an overnight stay in a barely-known woman's home.

He pasted on a fake smirk, needing to dissolve the blissful state of her features. "Are you ready to apologize for doubting my skills, Ella?"

The daze didn't fade. Instead, she smiled, those ruby lips making his dick twitch. "Hmm?"

He removed his fingers from her body and fought the need to lick away her arousal. "I'm waiting for you to admit you were wrong."

She chuckled. Breathy. Barely audible.

She was a pliable kitten.

He felt the same.

"I was wrong." She pushed to her elbows, then her knees. She straightened before him, putting her bra back in place, then glanced over her shoulder. "But it's five past nine. You didn't win the bet."

He could've talked his way out of it. Probably could've convinced her she'd been lying in a trance for more time than she had, but again, that amnesia had him questioning why he wanted to leave in such a hurry. "I guess I'm not quite as good as I thought I was."

She tilted her head, blinking up at him. He itched to loosen the top button of his shirt, to adjust his cock. She had him in all sorts of discomfort, and he'd be damned if he showed it.

"Are we done here?" She raised to her elbows.

"I don't know how to answer that."

She'd come. He'd felt it. Her pussy had spasmed around his fingers. More than once.

She'd bucked.

Writhed.

Shit. He needed to get the memory out of his head.

Her smile increased, her lashes still batting in a lazy, content rhythm. "It was a subtle way of asking if *you* were done." She pushed to her elbows, her thighs closing slightly. "I mean, can I return the favor?"

"*No*." God. No. The last thing he needed was to be force-fed more temptation. "This isn't a favor. This is..."

Torture. Pure and simple.

She stiffened, and finally that daze fled the scene like an Olympic sprinter.

He wanted to fuck her in so many ways he'd be able to publish a sex guide to rival the Kama Sutra. But before he did all that, he wanted to spank the look of rejection off her face. "Fucking you is a bad idea, that's all."

She nodded, sat up straight, and then swung her legs off the bed. "Don't elaborate. I've already taken the hint." She reached for her bedside table, pulled open the top drawer, and removed a large expanse of shiny black material. A robe.

In seconds, she was covered, her beautiful body hidden from view. She tied the thin belt around her waist with jerky movements, then clutched the lapels to hide her cleavage. "I'm going to freshen up. You don't have to hang around. I'm not going to hold you to the bet. Feel free to leave whenever you're ready."

He nodded, remaining silent as she strode for a door at the side of the room and closed herself in.

This was what he hated. The bullshit. The ping-pong match of hurt feelings and expectation. His dick didn't seem to care, though. The rock-hard part of his anatomy soldiered on, determined not to stand down until it glimpsed the front line.

He should leave.

It was the sensible option. He should walk out of here before she returned. No explanation. No goodbye.

He wouldn't have even contemplated his options if it were any other woman. He'd be out the door, down the hall, and driving back home without a second thought.

A toilet flushed, followed by a rush of tap water.

Leave or stay, Bryan? Leave or stay?

Shit.

It wasn't like she was an emotional threat. She had no interest in him. But why the fuck was he considering staying, anyway? For the bet? Maybe. He'd never backed out on a wager before. Problem was, he didn't know if it was more than that.

He closed his eyes and pinched the bridge of his nose. He was overthinking this when he shouldn't be thinking at all.

A cupboard closed in the adjoining room. The water stopped. The door reopened and the light spilling in from behind created a flawless silhouette. Her hair sat against her shoulders, the thin robe pulled tight at her waist. She looked like a model. One with beautiful curves and slightly faltering confidence.

"You're still here." She switched off the light and padded into the room.

He didn't bother fighting the laugh that escaped. "Yeah, sweetheart. Still here. I want to clear up the reason why fucking you is a bad—"

"Please don't." She held up a hand as she approached the bed. "I think I'm at my quota for your honesty."

He growled. If she didn't wipe the backslap of rejection off her face, he was going to do something he'd regret. Something they'd both regret. "The reason fucking you is a bad idea," he grated, "is because I can't sleep with a woman more than once."

Why *the fuck* had he said that?

She rolled her eyes and pulled back the coverings. "I also don't need a refresher on your rules. Shay gave me the Cliffs Notes."

He ground his teeth and wished he was the brute she thought he was. At least then he wouldn't feel obligated to give her an explanation.

"An incapability," he clarified. "*Not* a rule."

Her brows pulled together, the pinch of her forehead taking seconds, if not minutes. "You can't..."

"Get an erection? Wood? A hard-on? Whatever you choose to call it, I can't get it more than once for the same woman." He let the information sink in. The private, close-kept secret he'd never told a soul.

"Wow... So, you haven't slept with a woman more than once for how long?"

"Over twelve years."

"Holy. Shit." She drew out the words as she stared at him with a mix of fascination and concern. "Have you been to see anyone about it?"

"Oh, no." He shook his head. "Don't go thinking there's something wrong with my dick. There's no problem as far as I'm concerned. It's a skill. A talent that took years to master. It's my insurance policy."

"Insurance," she repeated slowly.

"Yeah, to protect the commitment phobia you seem to think I have."

"*Seem* to have?" Her lips quirked. "Is there really any doubt? You're seriously messed up."

"You won't hear a denial from me. But the reason for the explanation is to set things straight. The lack of fucking has nothing to do with you and everything to do with me needing to remain interested for the demonstration night."

She climbed onto the bed, her brow regaining its furrow.

"You know, Bryan, I never took you for the it's-not-you-it's-me type."

Because he wasn't. Never had been. She inspired anomalies. "And I never took you for a woman who could come with a mere twist of my fingers. I guess we both made inaccurate assumptions."

He kicked off his shoes and placed his socks inside them.

"You're still staying?"

"We made a bet. I'm not a sore loser."

This was a mistake. A huge mistake. His dick stood rigid as fuck. His restraint was equally vulnerable. Yet, for some unknown reason, he wasn't sprinting for the door.

He undid the top button of his shirt, moving down, one by one. Her hungry gaze ate up each new inch of exposed skin. He could practically feel those eyes sending their laser beam of fascination down his chest. The distraction should've made him stop and throw this upcoming train wreck in reverse.

"Want me to turn off the living room lights before I climb in?" He shoved the material off his shoulders, letting it fall to the floor.

"No." She shook her head. "It's early. I just want to lay here a while." She pulled the covers to her chin, snuggling farther into her pillow.

The entire scene before him seemed like a parallel universe. He didn't do this shit—not the sleepovers or the dinner. Definitely not the wine. And, Jesus Christ, if he thought about throwing the bet one more time, he'd probably throw his cookies, too.

But every time he blinked, he appreciated the sight he opened his eyes to. She looked natural. Relaxed. She didn't attempt to seduce him. She was just a woman, without flaw, and he was just a man, with many.

"So, who was she?"

He paused in the middle of unbuckling his belt. "She?"

"The woman who turned Bryan to Brute."

"There's no woman," he lied. "Like I said, I haven't been with anyone more than once since my school days." He released his belt, undid the zipper, and shoved his pants to the floor. "You really need to stop searching for excuses to explain who I am. There aren't any."

She made a noise. An *mmph* of disapproval. "We're all shaped by our experiences."

"If you say so." He averted his gaze, unable to look at her while he climbed into bed beside her. Out of all the sexual things he'd done over the years, this, by far, seemed the strangest.

Then again, it wasn't sexual.

This part was due to the bet.

A bet he'd thrown.

"If there's no woman, then tell me about your upbringing. Have you lived in Beaumont all your life? Do you have family here?"

Well, that was a sure-fire way to instigate a limp dick. "Grew up in Florida. Had a good education. Excelled in math and science. Hated my parents, like every kid my age." Problem was, his parents had hated him back.

"Do you go home often?"

"Not at all. A while ago I bought an apartment in Tampa, thinking I'd eventually revisit where I grew up. But..." What the fuck? This wasn't a shrink session. He didn't need to rehash the past to fill the silence. "I have no plans to go back now." He cleared his throat, rested back against the pillow, and stared up at the ceiling. "How 'bout you? What are your issues?"

"You already know mine." She released another noise, this time a tired moan. "Dead husband. Kinky proclivities. Inability to orgasm."

"You orgasm just fine."

Her chuckle was a puff of breath. "Spoken by the only man capable of making it happen."

"You'll figure yourself out soon enough." With another man. Maybe in another club.

"Yeah... I know."

He remained quiet through her long yawn, hoping she fell asleep and brought an end to the ocean-deep conversation.

He watched her from the corner of his eye, her hair splayed across the pillow, her blinks closing for longer and longer, until finally they closed for good. Tiny moans escaped her, the barely audible sounds sinking under his skin. His cock twitched again, the softened length making a comeback with renewed enthusiasm.

If she didn't stop, his ability to sleep would sit somewhere between not-likely and never-going-to-happen.

Not unless he took the edge off.

He stared at the clock, passing the whimper-filled minutes as he glared at those numbers. Each second provided a new rush of blood to his dick and a renewed sense that something was seriously off-kilter in this situation.

She hadn't tried to seduce him. She hadn't even stayed awake past ten o'clock.

He let out a silent puff of laughter. This woman was the best damn distraction he could ask for. But he couldn't stay here. Not in her bed, lusting over her with perversion while she slept. Nope, he needed to get up and disperse the blood pooling in his groin.

He slid from the mattress, his dick leading the way as he escaped down the hall, in search of...something.

There were innumerable offerings to appease his interest —the television remote, the magazines on the coffee table— and still, he found himself back at the bookshelf, his fingers skimming the spines of medical texts.

Even with the grim reaper hovering over his shoulder, his dick remained adamant. A trooper. The fucker had no plan to give up the fight.

He pulled the books from the shelf, one by one, and stacked them near the front door. She didn't want the reminder, and it wasn't like he had anything better to do. Apart from her. So, he kept going, his cheap workout continuing until every book on cancer sat waiting for him to leave.

And he *should* leave.

He hovered at the door, his issues resembling those of a teenager trying to sneak out for the first time.

"Fuck this." He wasn't a pussy. He could handle a sleepover. Especially when there were no claws sinking into his balls. She was asleep, for Christ's sake.

He padded back to the bookshelf, his attention snagging on the top shelf and the photos spaced evenly along the wood in silver frames. All the images were stereotypical happy families. Mother, daughter, and sister, in varying degrees of happiness.

Would their bubble ever burst, like his had?

He shook his head at the stupidity.

He'd never had a bubble to begin with. The script of his life had the fairytale set with a cast who never showed.

He slid two of the frames to the side and grabbed a shiny pink album stashed behind. He opened the cover, the pages flicking through his fingers, highlighting Ella in all her beaming glory. Her mother and sister played a leading role in the documentation of her life. But it looked like she'd hidden the shots of her husband. Or maybe those were reserved for the privacy of her bedroom.

There were birthday photos. Holiday happy snaps. More images with her sister. With Animals. At different locations. With sexy clothing. Then a fucking bikini.

He slammed the album shut and shoved it back onto the shelf. With every breath, he could taste her, smell her. His limbs tingled with the need to walk down that hall and give her what she'd asked for.

The one-fuck rule must have started to take its toll. The quality-over-quantity diet had turned him bat-shit crazy. So crazy he had to clench his fists to keep from palming his dick.

Alcohol. He needed alcohol.

He strode for the kitchen and grabbed the almost-empty wine bottle from her fridge. The lid was thrown aimlessly, the liquid contents sliding down his throat like the first taste of water after a year of dehydration.

He gulped. He chugged. He downed that motherfucker until the bottle was dry and he leaned against the sink, sucking in breath after breath. And still, his erection wouldn't admit defeat.

His mind was in on the act, too. Images of Ella flashed before his eyes. He could see her ass swaying as she dropped dishes in the sink. Could see her bending over to place food in the fridge.

He gripped the counter for grounding and pressed his erection against the cupboards, hoping to discourage the growing pulse.

The pressure increased.

He couldn't fight the need to palm himself through the thin material of his underwear, his fingers clutching tight. Every time he blinked, she was there—in the Vault, at the lockers, splayed beneath him on her bed. He heard her words, too. All those rasped pleas to be fucked. Hard. And the whimpers.

Jesus Christ.

He increased the severity of his hold, gripping his dick like he was trying to choke a snake. Damn thing wouldn't die.

The harder he squeezed, the better it felt. The pain was the best part.

One day, he'd return the favor. He'd torment her like she currently tormented him.

The tight grasp became a stroke, the first glide of friction bringing a heavy dose of pure relief. He bit his lower lip to stop a groan escaping and closed his eyes to concentrate on the childishness of his actions.

The darkness didn't help. Within seconds, he'd wrenched down his boxer briefs, leaving them to cup his balls as he spat on his hand. The first slide of his saliva-slicked palm was hell —pure torture and defeat, rolled into a package of fucking bliss.

Fighting was pointless. Instead, he squeezed his eyes tighter and punished the shit out of his dick, jerking it with harsh strokes, squeezing it with a tight fist. Back and forth he worked the length, each glide getting shorter. Sharper.

He growled through the pressure building in his balls, wanting to get this over and done with. He raised onto his toes, disgust turning his stomach as he blew his load in the sink. Burst after burst of white liquid shot from him, and still she didn't leave his mind. Pulse after pulse of release splattered the stainless steel, increasing his self-loathing, and all the while, she was still there.

Those eyes.

Those whimpers.

Those pleas.

He didn't understand it. Didn't want to.

"Fucking hell."

He rammed his softening dick into his underwear and washed his lack of restraint down the sink. This was Tera's fault. His family had shoved their way back into his life, destroying all the barriers he'd tried hard to erect.

Annihilating his sense of worth. His focus. Maybe even his confidence.

Bet or not, he had to leave.

If Ella woke and gave him another whispered proposition, he'd cave. He'd buckle like a cheap belt. And he didn't want to risk dragging anyone else into this regression.

He stalked into the living room, found a piece of paper and a pen, then scribbled his cell number in large font along with the message—*Next Thursday. 8 p.m. The Vault.*

He dropped the note beneath her glowing bedside lamp, tiptoed around the bed, and grabbed his pants off the floor. The loud clink of his buckle was a major "fuck you" from the universe. The noise shot through the silence and she whimpered in reply. He froze, pants halfway up his thighs, his dick beginning to reawaken like an energetic puppy.

"You're leaving?"

He tugged his pants to his waist, zipped, buttoned, and secured the belt. "Yeah. It's too damn early for me to sleep."

"Sorry." She turned toward him, cuddling her pillow as she blinked with lethargy. No woman had ever looked so feminine. So pliable. So breakable.

He only had to say the word and she'd be on her back, arms open, thighs spread. The thought should've been enough to turn him off.

Why didn't it?

Why was his blood rapidly regrouping in his dick?

He snatched his shirt off the floor and stabbed his arms through the sleeves with enough force to rip the material. Every second that drew closer to her proposition made his pulse quicken with anticipated relief. She was going to beg him to stay. She was singular breaths away from transforming into another groupie. Just like everyone else.

"Can you lock the door on your way out?" She stretched, the curve of her breasts straining against the sheet.

What. The. Fuck?

He frowned, confused by the awkward mix of beauty and rejection. "Sure." His fingers tripped over the remaining buttons. "I left a note on your coffee table. It's got my cell number on it. Message me if you've got any questions about the demonstration. Otherwise, I'll see you there."

"Who says I've made up my mind?"

"You'll be there, Ella. And you'll do a great job." He grasped his pockets, making sure he had his wallet, cell, and keys. "Thanks for tonight."

Thanks? For what? The erectile dysfunction and new kitchen fetish? Who the hell was he?

"Thanks?" She smiled. "Are you being polite again?"

"Nope." He made for the bedroom door, ready to run. "I got another cheap thrill and a boost to my ego. What's not to be thankful for?"

"Jerk," she whispered with sleep-addled humor.

And don't you forget it, sweetheart.

"Night, Ella." He stopped himself from turning back for one last look.

"Night, Brute."

The use of his nickname didn't escape him. She'd finally realized who he was. What he was. And even though hearing his title didn't bring the usual thrill, he knew the emotional distance would be nothing but a good thing.

CHAPTER TWELVE

The café's dining room was empty, spare a few women sharing their usual mid-afternoon coffee. The lull always hit hardest on Tuesday afternoons, which made for really crappy timing since Pamela's mind was mimicking an attention-starved toddler.

"Drop the dishcloth and nobody gets hurt."

Her hand paused mid-circular motion on the counter, and she glanced over her shoulder to see Kim holding the window spray as a weapon.

"What are you doing?"

"Mom and I have been patient, but your time is up. You need to stop the manic cleaning so we can have a serious conversation."

Pamela released the cloth and wiped her hands on the ass of her black leggings. "What have I done?"

"It's been two days."

"Two days," her mom parroted from the kitchen.

"Since?" She stalled, praying they weren't going to bring up the person she'd been trying desperately to forget. It had been two days since Brute. Two days since Chinese, orgasms, and a formidably sexy body in her bed.

"Don't play dumb." Kim crossed her arms over her chest. "We've given you space to digest whatever happened, and now we want the dirty details."

"Not today." She reclaimed her cloth and continued with the calming circular motions. "I don't want to talk about it."

"Since when?" Kim hissed. "You always tell me everything."

"Yeah...well, maybe it's time I stopped oversharing."

"Did he say something? Or do something?"

Pamela scoffed. "From now on, take that as a given. But after the other night, I've got bigger problems than his insults."

"I knew it." Her mother shoved through the swinging kitchen doors. "I never would've picked it from such a handsome boy, but I told Kim I had a niggling feeling about those marks on your throat."

"Mom," her sister warned. "We discussed this and decided it was a rash."

Oh. Shit.

Pamela's hand instinctively snapped to her neck, covering the thin scarf strategically placed around the fading red fingermarks.

"Or am I wrong?" Kim went from chastisement to fire and brimstone with the widening of her eyes. "Did he force himself on you?"

"No. *God*, no." How did she admit to loving every second of his strong hold around her throat? How could she make them understand she'd never been more turned on than in that moment? "The marks are..."

"Damn it, Pamela. Just tell us what happened." Her mother's concern came with a volatile voice. "Is everything okay?"

"Yes." She sucked in a breath and slumped with the exhale. She'd been dodging this conversation for a while. "Actually, no." She didn't want to admit what happened—the monumental stupidity. Problem was, she knew this drill. They weren't going to leave her alone until she blurted the truth. "I fell for him."

They stared.

Unmoving.

Unblinking.

"It's idiotic, I know." She winced through the words. "It must be something hormonal."

"I thought you said he was a dick." Kim lowered her voice and did a visual scan of the few remaining customers.

"He is." *Oh, God, he is.*

"Then there must be a reason."

There were many. The pathetic excuses swiftly formed a list in her mind—his touch, his voice, his body. He was gorgeous—*oh, so, gorgeous*—with his tough-man beard, scrutinizing eyes, and talented hands. Visually, he was perfection. And those books. He'd cleared the shelf that had served as a constant reminder of the months of cancer and misplaced hope. The realization had brought tears, happy ones.

And sad ones, too.

"I can see your brain running a mile a minute." Kim narrowed her eyes. "He did something to win you over, didn't he?"

"No. Not really." Definitely nothing worthy of the plaguing heart palpitations she'd been battling. "He was the same asshole, for the most part."

"And the other parts?" Her mom reached over the counter, tidying the sugar packets in an unconvincing act to appear unfazed. "Could there have been a deeper connection on some other level, maybe?"

Pamela rolled her eyes. "Wow. You slid off your protective suit and seamlessly pulled on a matchmaker cloak in record speed."

"I'm not matchmaking," her mom scoffed. "I'm only suggesting there may have been more of a connection between you than you think."

"Come on." Kim waved her on with a swirl of her hand. "Break it down. Tell us what happened. Start to finish."

Her mom cleared her throat. "Apart from the juicy stuff, of course."

"Of course." Jesus Christ. If she ever heard the word 'juicy' from her mother's lips again it would be too soon. Especially when referring to sex.

Her sister and mother had continuously supported her. They had her back even though they didn't understand her enjoyment of adult clubs or any of the facets within them. They listened without judgment. The only thing they didn't do was hide their confusion over it.

"He turned up at my apartment with food and wine. I think there may have even been a smile on his face." Yes, there'd definitely been a smile. A self-assured curve of his lips. "We talked over dinner, and he was friendly. Even a little funny. Then he helped clear the table and gave me a foot massage."

He'd shown his charm and more of that willingness to physically please. And one by one, the opposing list of negative attributes had begun to diminish under the weight of his allure.

"A foot massage? Is that a fetish thing?"

"There's no foot fetish." Not that she knew of. "He was being nice. He even opened up to me about a family struggle he's having."

Kim's brows pinched. "Then maybe you fell in love with him because—"

"Oh, no. No, no, no. This is *not* love." She snatched the dishcloth and twisted it in her hands. This thing wasn't anywhere close to the L-word. It didn't even nudge the edge of the greedy emotion. What she felt for Brute was something less vulnerable...but equally cloying.

"Then how hard was the fall?"

Pamela turned to scrub at a non-existent mark on the counter. "I don't know. Maybe it's nothing. There hasn't been anyone in my life since Lucas. Not other than physically." But he'd shown her a glimmer of the man beneath the mask. He'd given her a peek at the soft, gooey center, and it kinda seemed comparable to her favorite peppermint-filled chocolate. "This could be a simple case of enjoying the attention I've been starved of. I just wish I could get him out of my head. I need to stop thinking about him."

"Because he's allergic to commitment?"

She paused, wondering if her situation would be as dire if that was the only issue. "Because I'm supposed to be his assistant for this demonstration night, and I'm not sure I can hide the way I feel. The last time I showed any sort of interest, he confronted me about it in front of the entire club. I've never been more humiliated, and back then, I didn't think of him as more than an asshole. Imagine how he'd react now."

Kim cringed.

"See?" It was a problem. A big problem.

"Tell him you can't help with the class thingy," her mother offered. "Call and say you're busy."

"If I call him, he'll expect an explanation." And if they spoke, she'd cave under the dominance in his voice.

"Then don't call." Kim shrugged. "Send a message saying something came up and you can't make it. Don't elaborate. Give him the bare minimum details and leave it at that. You don't owe him anything."

No. She supposed she didn't. Aside from a one-sided orgasm tally, there was no commitment or binding agreement.

"Where's your phone?" Kim glanced beneath the counter, pushing aside her mother's handbag.

"Under the register."

Her sister scooted farther along, retrieved the device, and handed it over. "Send it now."

Pamela sucked in a slow breath and eyed her mother, who nodded in solemn agreement. "Do you really think this is the best way to go about it?" Guilt took over her stomach, making it roil and rumble. Or maybe that was the fear of missing out on another life-changing orgasm.

"Do you have his number?" Kim asked.

"Yeah." She'd saved his details under Brute. Not Bryan. She'd even quit using his name in the hope the reminder of his attitude would kick her out of her stupidity.

The plan had turned out to be highly ineffective.

"Go on." Kim spurred her on with the jut of her chin. "Do it."

Pamela lowered her gaze to the cell in her hand and typed without thought. If she paused, even for a second, she wouldn't go through with it.

Something came up. I can't be at the Vault next Thursday. I'm sorry.

She clicked send and swallowed over the squeeze in her chest. *Bye, bye, beautiful orgasms.* "There." She handed the device to Kim. "Done."

It didn't feel *done.* Her heart beat in a fractured tempo. Her chest grew heavy. She hadn't liked a man in years. She hadn't felt anything apart from pure frustration toward the opposite sex since Lucas died. Which made shoving Brute away seem comparable to punching herself in the vag.

"I'll silence the ringer." Kim pressed buttons on the

screen, then returned it to its place under the counter. "If he calls, ignore it. If he messages, delete it. You don't need another emotionless ass in your life."

Ouch. The insult hit her in the chest. "Lucas wasn't an ass."

"No, sweetie." Her mom gave a sad smile. "But he didn't love you either. You deserve something better this time."

Yeah, she knew she did. Her problem was her inability to attract anything other than two distinct categories of men—those who could work her body into a frenzy and leave her heart stone-cold or those who warmed her heart and lacked any understanding of her sexuality.

"Come on." Kim inclined her head in the direction of the dining room. "Help me clear these tables to get your mind off him. And while we're at it, I can tell you about those online dating sites I've been researching."

She established a routine for the remaining two hours of her shift—do five minutes' work, check her phone, ponder why Brute hadn't responded, then do another five minutes' work. The cycle was vicious. Then again, maybe his lack of response was a relief.

"See? There was nothing to worry about." Kim flicked off the kitchen lights and headed for the front door. "He probably doesn't care at all."

Her mother had said the same thing before she'd finished for the day.

"Yeah. Maybe."

Brute didn't seem like a man who wouldn't care about a cancellation. Or more specifically, a rejection. He seemed the type to demand explanations and berate unworthy responses. "At least I'll sleep better tonight."

"Do you want to come over and watch a movie? We can get pizza."

"No, I'm good." Pamela pulled the café keys from her handbag as her sister opened the front door. "I think a bath and an early night is what I need."

She stepped onto the sidewalk, dragging the door shut behind her. With a jab of the key and the flick of her wrist, the lock was secure and she could finally go home.

"Sorry to interrupt, ladies."

She turned at the unfamiliar male voice and found a dose of cuteness staring back at her. "Muffin Man."

Kim snorted at her side.

"Muffin Man?" His hope-filled expression fell.

"Sorry." She slapped a hand over her mouth and tried to ignore the heat setting her cheeks to flame. "I... Um..."

"You're a regular." Kim chuckled. "But we didn't know your name. So, Pamela dubbed you Muffin Man."

"I did *not*." It had been Kim. All Kim.

The guy glanced between them, a smile gently spreading his lips. "It's Callum." Humor tinged his voice, friendly and sweet.

Too friendly and sweet. If only he had a fierce streak, then her uterus would be doing tumbles.

"Nice to meet you, Callum." Kim backtracked, removing herself from the equation with stealthy finesse. "But I'm going to have to run." She finger-waved. "I have an appointment with my personal trainer. I'll talk to you later, sis."

Pamela glared at her lying sister's back until she lost sight of her in the busy foot traffic. When she turned to Callum, he was staring at her, his brown eyes filled with nervousness.

"Well, it's great to formally meet you, Callum. Was there something I could help you with?"

He rubbed the back of his neck. Nibbled his bottom lip.

The apprehension may have been endearing to someone else, but she'd always admired confident men.

"Yeah, I've been hanging around, waiting for you to finish for the day. I thought, maybe, I could buy you a drink or two."

"Oh." Her brain seized. "Um..." She hadn't been expecting an invitation. Especially not from a man who seemed puppy-like in his timid nature. "I..."

"I know it's out of the blue." He gave an embarrassed chuckle. "It's taken a while to work up the guts to speak to you."

Again, she should've been charmed. Even a little flattered. He seemed like a nice guy.

Evidently, her libido didn't do nice.

"Tonight?" She glanced along the pavement, caught between voicing a gentle dismissal to appease her disinterest, and an unwanted acceptance which would finally see her sampling a different sort of male.

Who knew? Maybe this timid guy had the occasional anal orgasm in his repertoire.

"I, umm..." She focused on the people passing by—the businessmen, the couples, the kids. Now was as good a time as any to try something new, right?

She opened her mouth, poised to accept, when her gaze snagged on the man leaning against his car a few yards down the street. As if pulled from her fantasies, Brute stood there, arms crossed over his chest, his stance casual as he pinned her heart like a preserved butterfly.

"I'm sorry, Callum." She turned back to meet soft brown eyes. "I can't tonight."

He shrugged, his smile now painted on. "That's okay. I know it's late notice. Maybe another night?"

"Sure." Who knew what the future held? One day soon

she seriously had to quit the infatuation with emotionless men and fall for someone like Callum.

Someone sickeningly sweet and drama-free.

Just not today. Not when a man entirely opposite stood close by, invigorating her bloodstream with his annoyance.

"Have a good night." Callum inclined his head in farewell, waved, then turned in those big workman boots.

"You, too." She plastered herself against the glass doors, refusing to look at the man who approached. The closer Brute came, the harder it became to breathe. Her skin prickled. Her throat tightened.

"Is he the reason you're leaving me high and dry?" he growled in greeting.

Her heart beat harder, the mix of attraction and his anger sizzling all her nerves. "What are you doing here?"

"I thought I deserved an explanation."

"You could've called."

"I thought the same about you. After the orgasms I've dished out, you'd think the last thing I deserved was a few vague words via text."

Oh, boy.

Mentally, she had her hands on his shoulders, pulling him in for a harsh kiss that would end with her knee in his junk. Physically, though, she had her teeth clenched and a scowl firmly in place.

Nothing about this moment could end well. Especially when she couldn't voice the real reason for her cancellation, and she didn't have a fake excuse on stand-by.

"So, I'll ask again." He beamed down at her. "Is that guy the reason you're leaving me high and dry?"

She wrinkled her nose. "No."

"You dating him?"

"Is that any of your business?"

"If you keep coming to me complaining you can't get

fucked properly, then, yeah. It sure is, 'cause that guy is never going to do you right."

"Keep coming to you?" God, this man made her blood boil and her pussy contract, all at the same time. "You want an explanation for why I canceled? Maybe check your attitude."

"Bullshit. You've always known my attitude. If it's not that guy, my next guess is your husband."

Her mouth gaped at the insertion of Lucas into the conversation.

Seconds ago, Callum made her flat-line with disinterest. In a heartbeat, this callous man had given her a major case of arrhythmia.

"The other night," he continued, "you said you hadn't had anyone over since he'd died. So, if it's not the pretty boy, I'm guessing it's a guilt thing."

"This *is not* a guilt thing," she grated.

"Then what?"

She sucked in a deep breath, let it out slowly, and fought against the warring emotions bubbling in her chest. She hated this sparring match. Loved it, too. She wanted to claw his eyes out. Wanted to fuck his brains out. This situation was a whirlwind of confusion.

"I already told you I need to give up the Vault. Going back for one last time is a stupid idea."

"Instead, you expect this new guy to rock your world?" He ran a rough hand over his beard, his scowl unwavering. "You're making the wrong decisions."

"And you're an expert on love now?"

He screwed up his perfectly perfect face. "I'm not talking about love. This is about fucking. You can't seriously believe that guy would have the first clue about getting you off."

"They say it's the quiet ones you need to look out for."

"They're wrong." He stepped forward, getting in her face,

a mere breath away. "The quiet ones bring shock value because they're boring as hell. What you need is someone who lives and breathes to fuck. A guy who can match your appetite. Someone who can push you. Test you. You don't need a guy who doesn't have the balls to tell you he'd like to see your sweet little cunt riding his dick all night."

She shivered. Head to foot. He stole her breath. Infused her with adrenaline. Oh, God, her panties were damp.

"Go home, Ella." He stepped away and made for his car, leaving her reeling with the abrupt end to the conversation. "Get dressed and meet me out in front of your building at nine."

"Excuse me?" Her hands shook. Her brain stopped firing on all cylinders. There were many things to hate about his statement—the authority, the self-righteousness. Yet, her libido only focused on the sexy dominance. "Why?"

"I'm taking you out. It's about time somebody taught you how to find the right hook-up."

A whimper formed low in her chest. *Reject, reject, reject.* She couldn't go ahead with this. She refused. "Don't worry about me. I know what I'm doing."

"Your history at the Vault proves otherwise." He pulled open the driver's door and looked at her over the roof of his shiny car. "Nine, Ella. Be ready."

Then he was gone, leaving her to become overwhelmed by excitement and pure, undiluted fear.

CHAPTER THIRTEEN

Five past nine came soon enough for Bryan not to have to think too much about what the hell he'd instigated. He had better things to do than teach a woman how to listen to her own instincts. But here he stood, leaning against his car, in front of her building while he stared at his watch.

He didn't expect her to be early. Didn't even anticipate she'd be on time. She'd need to retaliate, at least a little, before she gave in and realized she wasn't going to find the right guy without assistance.

She needed his help, maybe even wanted it. The confusing part was why he gave a shit. He supposed he didn't like anyone leaving the Vault unsatisfied. The low enjoyment rating came as a personal blow as much as a professional one. And he still needed her assistance for the demonstration.

So, technically, this was business.

He'd scratch her back. She'd scratch his.

She was also a distraction. The only thing capable of keeping his mind off Tampa, family, and throat-clogging hate. Annoying Ella made the other shit in his life disappear. At least temporarily. The time alone, backed up against his car, made all the thoughts flood to the forefront.

He stared at the yellow glow from the window he guessed was hers and waited for the lights to fade.

They didn't.

Not after one minute. Not even after five.

His cell vibrated in his back pocket, the intrusion a mental *and* physical pain in his ass, but a better source of entertainment than a pane of glass. He pulled out the device, scowled at Leo's name, and pressed connect. "Yeah?"

"Shay thinks you're high on the latest designer drug because of your unnaturally good mood this afternoon. What gives?"

Bryan thought back on the last six hours and refused to acknowledge what might have made a big enough change in his attitude for someone to notice. There was only one thing. More specifically, one person. "I've been testing a new powder on the market," he drawled. "I thought about selling it on the sly to the younger ravers."

There was more than a beat of silence. "You're joking, right?"

"What do you want, Leo? I'm busy."

"Doing what?"

"Your mother. So, if you don't mind, it's time to lube up."

"Fucking Shay," Leo muttered. "I don't know why she thought you were acting oddly cheery lately. You're still the same asshole you've always been."

Bryan grinned. This was how they rolled. Their friendship grew with the help of cheap shots and quick comebacks. "Is that the only reason for the call?"

"No. I wanted to know what steps you've taken to fix the issue in the Vault."

"I'm working on it." He kept staring at Ella's window and

wondered about the seductive possibilities of what she might be wearing.

"How? I need details. Cassie and T.J. want an update."

"I told you Ella would do the demonstration, and she will." He swallowed, clearing the dryness from his throat. For once, confidence didn't coat his tone. His words fell flat under uncertainty. "I'll confirm the deal tonight."

"Confirm the deal? Is that what the kids are calling it these days?" Leo chuckled. "She's the reason for the drug high, isn't she? Does the big, bad Brute have a crush?"

Bryan scowled, wishing the look could make its way through to Leo's phone. "This big, bad Brute is going to crush your face if you don't leave me alone to fix this mess."

The chuckle turned into unrestrained laughter. "I nailed it, didn't I? You like this woman."

"Of course," Bryan grated. "You nailed it just as hard as I'll nail Shay the next time you work a late shift."

The delirious mirth increased. "Are you on a date?"

"Goodbye, Leo."

"It *is* a date."

Bryan disconnected the call and pocketed the cell. Ten seconds passed before the first text message vibrated from his back pocket. Then another and another.

Fucking Leo.

The squeak of the apartment building door disturbed the night air, and he lifted his gaze to find Ella's familiar silhouette exiting the lobby. The outside lights bore down on her, giving him an unforgiving view of the skin-tight red dress that ensured no man would need the use of his imagination tonight.

Her blonde hair danced over her shoulders, along with a white scarf trailing into the deep-V of her cleavage revealing a mass of creamy skin, while her cherry-stained lips matched her seductive stiletto heels. But it was her eyes

130

that slayed him, and the nervous sweep of her lashes, exposing the slightest need for validation as she approached.

"You're late," he muttered.

"You're lucky I'm here at all."

Her stride didn't falter as he pushed from the car and opened the passenger door. "If you didn't show, I would've figured out a way into your building and dragged you out myself."

"I know. That's the only reason I came."

"Sure it is." He didn't believe her for a second. Not when she'd gone to so much effort to look drop-dead gorgeous. Every inch of her made his cock fill with interest. Especially those heels.

If he were the one taking this woman home tonight, he'd make sure those shoes remained firmly in place while he sank between those thighs. She'd be splayed across his bed, completely naked, all bar those ruby, fuck-me stilettos.

And hadn't that image just given his dick the green-light to adolescence.

"Nice heels," he grunted.

"Thanks. You look good, too." Her sarcasm was flamboyant, letting him know his compliment about her shoes was far from worthy. "I like the suit. I bet it's a carbon copy of every other one you've worn for the last five years."

He beat back a grin. "You can't ditch a classic."

She stopped in front of him, placing her hand-held clutch to her hip. "No. But it wouldn't hurt to change things up a bit. You're starting to look like a control freak with the constant stiff-suit ensemble."

Stiff suit? Control freak?

She had no idea.

He stepped toward her, hovering close, dragging her sweet scent of lust and beauty deep into his lungs. "You ain't seen nothin', sweetheart. Imagine how wet those panties would get if you had a full dose of my control."

She chuckled, batting away his arrogance with a sly tilt of her lips. "Well, we better not test that theory." She pushed past him, pausing to whisper, "Because I'm not wearing any panties."

He snapped his mouth shut and took the sucker punch to his balls head on. She was messing with him. He knew it. She knew it.

It didn't stop his gaze from landing on her ass in search of a panty line, though. A non-existent panty line.

Get a fucking grip.

He wasn't going there. Not tonight.

"Get in." He made his way around the car and yanked open his door.

This excursion was about teaching her how to read men. To determine the wheat from the chaff. The sexually experienced from the ignorant.

She needed to trust him, not only to get her laid, but to change her mind about the demonstration night. Time was running out, along with his patience, and there was no way he could miss next Thursday's session in the Vault. He needed to be between those sordid walls. He craved the grounding. The connection.

And, if he was being honest, he wanted to see if the image of Ella, naked and in front of a crowd, was as perfect in real life as it was in his mind.

If he fucked her now, his limp-dick insurance policy would steal all that away from him. The class wouldn't run with the enthusiasm it deserved. His interest in her would plummet, if not vanish entirely. There'd be no buzz. No thrill.

He'd make a fool of them both.

This constant state of arousal around her would work much more favorably. His intuition would be flawless with his current level of interest. All he had to do was keep riding this wave of erection-inducing torture until next week. Then he'd reward himself with one hot and heavy fuck and be done with her.

His insurance policy would make sure of it.

He slid into the driver's seat and shut the door behind him. "You ready?"

"Do I have a choice?" She ran a hand down her thigh, straightening non-existent wrinkles in her dress. "Where are we going, anyway?"

"To a bar not far from here." He started the ignition and pulled onto the street. "I know the guy who owns the place."

"Will there be music and dancing?"

He could see her cleavage from the corner of his eye. The lush curves were enough to drive him to distraction. "You don't want music. Dance floors are for guys looking for an easy lay. What you need is someone willing to hold a conversation. If they don't bother learning who you are, they won't bother learning what you want."

"But I like dancing."

And his dick loved the thought of seeing those hips sway. "Not tonight, you don't."

She sighed and rested her head against the passenger window. "If you say so."

"Yeah," he muttered. "I say so."

The drive was quiet, the soft hum of her voice underlining every song on his playlist. This time he itched to fill the void. He had questions. He had suggestions. But every time he thought of something to say, he fell into a pathetic hole where he analyzed the necessity of every word.

He questioned himself.

Over her.

What the hell?

"So..." He pushed through the analytical crap like a

motherfucker and focused instead on his building jealousy. "The guy from this afternoon, are you seeing him?"

Her head snapped around. "What guy? Callum? No." The questions shot at him. "He's a regular at the cafe. This afternoon was the first time he's spoken anything other than a drink order to me."

"He asked you out, right?" He hadn't needed to hear the words to read the man's shit-scared demeanor. "What did you say?"

"Why do you care?"

"I don't. I'm only trying to get a feel for how you vet potential lovers."

She focused out her window and spoke softly. "I politely declined."

"Good." The guy wasn't her type. Anyone with a spine as languid as a snake would be an unworthy match for her. She craved strength and dominance. Not a hesitant guy who rocked from foot to foot while talking to his crush.

"For now," she added. "I think I might need to reassess after tonight."

"Why?" He maneuvered through the light traffic, taking in side-glances of her as he went. "What's going to happen tonight?"

"I don't know." She shrugged. "I think I need to stop focusing all my attention on a sexual connection. It's time to lean more toward a mental bond."

"That sounds dreamy," he drawled. "Let me know how it feels when your hymen grows back."

She gave a breathy snicker. "You're such a dick. Just because you enjoy solitude doesn't mean everyone else has to."

"One doesn't have to be the loneliest number. To me, it's the most reliable."

"We'll have to agree to disagree." She shot a glance over her shoulder, giving a quick inspection of the car's interior.

He held his breath and clenched the steering wheel when her eyes widened. For fuck's sake. Why couldn't he catch a break?

"You kept the books?" she asked.

"Yeah."

"I wasn't sure if you were going to keep them to read or—"

"I'm not. I planned on throwing them in the nearest dumpster, but turns out those books are fucking expensive. I read the price sticker on the back of one and couldn't bring myself to trash them. So, I'm waiting for a spare afternoon to drop them at an oncology ward. Or somewhere else they might be of use."

She didn't reply for long seconds that felt like unending months. In that head of hers, he figured she was creating a punishing reply.

"You had no intention of reading them, but you took them anyway?"

He ground his teeth.

"Thank you, Bryan."

Shit. Shit. *Shit*.

She was back to using his name.

"Don't mention it," he muttered and wanted to back it up with, "No, really, don't fucking mention it. *Ever*."

"You can be a sweet guy, you know that?"

"Yeah. The perfect gentleman," he mocked. "Especially when I have my hands around your throat and your tight cunt around my finger."

She gave a breathy chuckle. "Are you trying to shock me with dirty talk?" She clucked her tongue. "Amateur."

He was. Around her, at least.

"It's hardly dirty talk." He turned onto their street,

thankful for the upcoming escape from the confined space. "I should give you a lesson on that, too." No. *No,* he couldn't. What the hell was he thinking?

She sighed and remained quiet.

Crisis averted.

Thank fuck.

"We're almost there." The looming threat of rain had made for less foot-traffic. Not many people were around. Then again, it was nine on a Tuesday night. Not really the hour for raving. "This is the place."

He took in the two-story building as he turned into the parking lot entrance. The front facade had received a facelift since he'd last been here. The dark brick was now matched with black guttering, giving a Gothic feel, while the warm yellow lights brightened up the interior.

"You like it here?" She fumbled with the ends of her scarf.

"Yeah. It's a low-key version of Shot of Sin."

"How so?"

"There's booze, soft music, and rooms for hire upstairs." He parked at the back of the lot and cut the engine.

"Rooms for...?"

"Privacy. Playing. Fucking. You name it." He turned to her, taking in the slight hitch to her chin and her sharp inhale. The mental image had turned her on, which meant his dick wanted in on the action. "Are you ready?"

She held up her clutch and nodded. "All set."

His palms began to sweat as he took in all the visible assets other men would soon be ogling. "Lose the scarf."

Her mouth gaped. "Why?"

Because I want to see more of you. "It doesn't match the dress." *And every time you touch it I think about tying you to my bed.*

Her hand shot to her throat. "I need to wear it."

"Because?"

Her lips worked around silent words before she sighed. "Because I have marks on my neck that I couldn't cover with make-up."

He scowled. "A rash?"

"No." Her focus shot to his. "I'm talking about your fingermarks all over my skin."

"I hurt you?" Snapshots of remembrance peppered his vision—his hands around soft flesh, her moans, the involuntary spasms of her pussy.

He closed his eyes and ran a hand over his face. *Don't think about it. Don't picture it. Just forget the whole scarf thing and get the fuck out of this suffocating space.*

"Not enough," she murmured.

Jesus. It was time to bail.

"Good." He shoved open his car door and escaped the confines of the car.

She followed and met his gaze over the roof. "Do you understand why I have to wear it now?"

"Yeah." He didn't need a reminder staring him in the face all night long, either. "It looks fine."

He didn't watch her as he slammed his door. He didn't need to confirm an eye roll accompanied her scoff; he was already sure of it.

"You realize *fine* is far from a compliment." She shut her door and rounded the hood. "Just for future reference, I mean."

It wasn't like he lacked the ability to compliment her.

He could praise the ever-loving fuck out of her if he wanted. He could tell her how the mere peripheral vision of her gave his dick an aneurism. He could point out how perfect those breasts were—plump and full. Or count on his fingers the amount of times he'd wanted to bend her over different objects and fuck the frustration from his system.

Didn't mean those words would ever pass his lips, though.

"Duly noted."

He started for the front of the building, the gravel of the parking lot rolling under his soles. She wobbled with her first step, her thin heels losing traction.

"You okay?" The instinct to reach out and secure an arm around her waist was a mistake. Yet another idiotic move when it came to this woman.

"You don't need to hold onto me." She inched forward. "I can manage."

He didn't doubt it. But now he had the feel of her embedded into his side, and he wasn't willing to let go. He could smell her hair, the floral scent more of an aphrodisiac than a gut full of oysters. "I insist."

He held her gaze, catching every flicker in her expression as he tightened his hold. She swallowed. Straightened. Lifted her chin. Those lashes even beat with timid lethargy.

"Doesn't it defeat the purpose of trying to pick up another man if I walk in with your hands on me?"

He didn't care. "Doesn't falling face first into the gravel and skinning your knees defeat the purpose of that sexy dress?"

She blinked. Balked. Gaped.

He had no clue why.

"Sexy dress?" One perfectly shaped brow arched.

He huffed and ignored the grin spreading those red lips. "Come on." He led her forward, her waist burning a hole through his palm, until he dropped his grip at the start of the sidewalk. "Have you got it from here?"

"I always had it, Brute." She strutted those toned legs in front of him, making her way to the entrance before he snapped out of his stare and quickly caught up.

"Where do you want to sit?" She glanced around the room, eyeing the booths along the back wall, then the cushion-lined sofas near the front windows, her attention finally coming to rest at the stools lining the bar. "Should we stay close to the booze?"

"That sounds like a good idea." A fucking brilliant plan.

She continued forward while he hung back, waiting in case those gravity-defying heels slipped out from beneath her as she slid onto the closest stool.

"So, tell me your type." He positioned himself beside her and swung around to face the room. It took less than five seconds to deem every guy here as an unworthy conquest. "What are you looking for?"

"Well..." She followed, placing her back to the bar. "Sexually speaking, I want someone confident and—"

"I know what you need sexually." The reminder was a mental stroke along his dick. "What are you after outside the bedroom? I'm talkin' looks, income, race, religion."

"None of that matters to me."

"Looks don't matter?" He raised a fuck-off brow. "Looks always matter."

She shrugged and jutted her chin to the left. "The guy in the back is attractive."

"The one with the Van Dyke beard?"

"Yeah. I don't mind a bit of facial scruff."

His hand itched with the need to palm his jaw. He'd bet she'd prefer a full beard when it was grazing the sensitive flesh of her inner thighs. "How about his wedding ring? Does that bother you?"

Her nose wrinkled, her gaze snapping to his. "How did you even notice that?"

"It's not what you notice, it's what you need to look for. Wedding bands or a tan line on the appropriate finger are a good place to start."

She nodded and sat up straight, ever the eager student. "What else?"

He became fascinated by the way her attention strayed

around the room, scoping potential lovers. "The guy you're looking for will be paying you attention. Watching you. Trying to work you out before you even notice him."

Just like I am.

She continued with her search, her shoulders drooping moments later. "Well, I guess I'm out of luck." She turned to face him. "Nobody in here is looking at me."

He wasn't going to prove her wrong. Pointing out all the men who'd already mentally stripped that dress from her body was a conversation for later. When he'd had enough time to determine who would be the right fit for her. "It's early. Don't give up yet."

She nodded, the defeat still a slight groove between her brows. He itched to smother the expression. Wipe it away. With his hands, his mouth, his dick.

Goddammit.

"What do you want to drink?" He yanked his gaze away and raised a hand to call the bartender.

"Tequila sunrise, please."

He placed the order and focused on the drink preparation to ensure he didn't drag her ass out of here for his own fulfillment. He'd already started contemplating the possibility of a different demo assistant. Someone who could take Ella's place so he could sate the rabid hunger tonight and let his insurance policy kick in before this got out of hand.

He didn't care about the female Vault members boycotting the class. Or how Leo and T.J. would want to kill him. All the reasons from needing her assistance disappeared under the chokehold of lust.

His level of investment in this woman was too fucking high. He was beginning to enjoy being around her. The rollercoaster rise and fall of her smile kept stealing his attention. And that dress...

Shit. This wasn't right.

"What's wrong?" she asked. "You look like you're sulking. If you want to go home..."

Take the offer. Get out of here. "We're not leaving."

"Then cheer up, buttercup. You're scaring away any potentials." She waggled her brows and the sultry curve of her lips pummeled another meaty fist into his crotch.

"Here you go." The bartender slid over their drinks.

"Thanks." He snatched at his beer and enjoyed the liquid solace gliding down his throat. He needed to take the edge off. To snuff the burn.

"What's the craziest thing you've done, Brute?" Ella nibbled on the straw sticking from her drink, her head cocked as those eyes bore through him. "I bet you've got a lot of stories to tell."

He shrugged. "Nothing comes to mind."

"You own a sex club and nothing comes to mind?"

He took another long pull of beer. Conversation became difficult—the grasp for coherence almost impossible when her lips were a tempting breath away. "Sex isn't crazy. It's natural. People have been screwing since the dawn of time. What I find hard to justify are those who skydive or participate in adrenaline-fueled sports." He pointed a finger at her. "Or those who get married. Now, if you ask me, making a commitment like that is fucking insane."

She stared at the bar, a far-off gleam in her eyes as she smiled. "My marriage was far from conventional."

"Why is that?"

Her lips parted and silent words hovered out of reach until she sighed. "Hold on a sec." She leaned forward and focused on the bartender. "Excuse me. Can I get a shot of tequila, please?"

"Shots?"

Her fingers tapped against the bar, her leg jolted.

"Have I missed something?" he asked.

She gave a bark of laughter and grasped the shot glass sliding toward her. She downed the contents in one winced gulp and kept her focus on the bartender. "You might want to fill that up again, please. I think I'm going to need it."

"What's going on?" He didn't like the change in her demeanor. He also didn't like the rapid approach of lowered inhibitions. He was already battling enough for them both.

She licked her lower lip, sweeping the remnants of alcohol away. "There was no commitment when I married."

"You had an open relationship?" Her husband must have been one laidback motherfucker. To share a woman as beautiful as Ella was a risk. You'd never know when another guy would throw club etiquette to the wind and steal her right out from beneath you.

"It's a long story."

"Then hurry up and get on with it."

She eyed him, up and down.

Shit. He pulled back, unsure when he'd inched close enough to hear the hitch in her breath.

"Go on." He turned to the bar, palmed his beer, and took a gulp. "We've got all night." At the very least, until he drowned his dick in liquor.

She fiddled with the refilled shot glass, running her finger around the rim. "I met Lucas on one of those European bus holidays. I was doing the touristy thing with Kim, and he was traveling alone. We got to talking and eventually hooked up. It wasn't anything romantic. Just sex." Her shoulders slumped with a deep exhale. "*Amazing* sex."

"I get the picture."

"No, you don't." She spoke to the glazed wood of the bar. "I'd never been with anyone like him before. He taught me things. He knew my body better than I did, which was strange because we rarely spoke. He kept to himself a lot and we only caught up at night."

Bryan gripped his beer, his focus on the liquid. For a fleeting second, his chest constricted with jealousy, but he doused that fucker with the remainder of his drink and quickly ordered another with the raise of a finger.

"When the tour ended, we went our separate ways and neither one of us looked back. I didn't ask for his number, and he showed no interest in keeping in contact. At least, not until he turned up on my doorstep a few months later."

Made sense. The guy must've realized his mistake. Ella was a different sort of woman. Sexually confident and inquisitive. A catch. Anyone who let her walk deserved to wallow in regret.

"Couldn't live without you, huh?" He welcomed his new beer with a deep pull, determined to douse the discomfort under his sternum.

"Actually ..." Her voice turned somber. "He told me he wouldn't be living at all in the near future. He found out about the cancer a few weeks after he returned from Europe."

Bryan dropped his glass to the bar and turned to her.

"It wasn't the happiest of reunions." She shrugged. "But I'm glad he found me."

"That's when you got married?"

"Pretty much. He didn't want to die alone, and I didn't want that for him either. He deserved to have someone by his side."

"What about his family or friends? Couldn't they have looked after him? You said the two of you barely spoke."

"Apart from work colleagues, Lucas didn't have anyone to rely on. His mother had health problems of her own back in Chicago. He didn't even tell her about the cancer. She thought he was going on another vacation. Instead, he came to find me."

"*Jesus.*" He blindly swiped for his beer and knocked back

another gulp. "That's a lot of pressure to put on a stranger." The guy seemed like a dick. A selfish, emotionless asshole.

"It was. But I was financially compensated. Our marriage became the equivalent of an employment contract. I quit my waitressing job to concentrate on his health, and when he passed, I became the sole beneficiary of everything he left behind."

She dipped her finger into the tequila, then sucked the moisture away. If their conversation hadn't been about cancer, chemo, and all things melancholy, he would've blown his load then and there.

"His money allowed me to buy this apartment and my cafe. It gave me the opportunity to help my sister who had mounting educational debts, and my mom who'd struggled since my father left. Not that they wanted anything to do with the inheritance. They disagreed with what I did."

"Because you were financially compensated?"

"No." She nibbled her bottom lip and shook her head. "Because at that point, Lucas and I weren't emotionally connected, and they knew it wouldn't end that way. They could see me falling for him, without those feelings being reciprocated."

His chest constricted, the building jealousy hitting harder the further they sank into this conversation. "And you put your life on hold anyway."

"And I'd do it again. There's no way I could've let him die alone. How could I live with myself if I let him walk away? I knew what I was getting myself into. I made the decision on my own." She shrugged. "In the end, they were right. I started hoping for more."

"More what? Time?"

"I don't know." She cringed. "Everything was complicated, especially with my extreme naivety. I've grown up a lot since then."

"Shit." He rested an elbow on the bar and looked at her. *Really* looked at her. "Didn't knowing the end game make it easier to close yourself off emotionally? At least to some extent?"

"How do you close yourself off emotionally, Bryan?" She met his stare. "How do you stop caring? God knows I couldn't figure out how."

She dipped her finger back into the tequila and swirled the contents with her fingertip. "Our days were spent between doctors' appointments and living out a fast-tracked bucket list. We also rekindled the physical relationship when he was able. It became hard building walls against something that monumental." She fell silent, stealing his fascination with each passing minute. "I ended up loving him... In my own little way."

He kept staring at her, kept blinking, kept breathing. He couldn't think past the need to do something, anything, to wipe the pained look off her face.

"Sorry." She winced. "I really won the award for Most Morbid Change in Conversation, didn't I?"

He swiped the shot glass out from beneath her hand and downed the contents in one regrettable swallow. "Yep. And now you're cut off." He cleared his throat to dissolve the burn. "You're a depressing drunk."

Her eyes widened, then a chuckle broke free. "Not usually." She nudged him with her elbow. "I blame the company I keep."

She could blame him all she liked, as long as the smile continued to stay plastered on those dark lips.

"Yeah, well, you need to shape up before your drinking privileges are returned."

"That's rich, coming from Mr. Moody."

"Moody? I'm pretty sure I stick to the one mood ninety percent of the time."

She quirked her lips as she pondered his response. "I guess you're right."

And just like that, her eyes lost the darkened shade of mourning and brightened to a mesmerizing blue.

"Okay." She rubbed her hands together. "Let's get this conversation back on track. We need to focus on getting me laid."

He palmed his beer as the added layer of history tugged at something other than his lust. The additional reminder of why they were here didn't fill him with warm and fuzzies, either. He didn't want to send her home with someone else. He didn't want to send her back to her apartment at all. "Maybe tonight's not the night for this."

"Of course it is." She grabbed his arm, those fingers searing skin and nerves. "Seriously, I need to get lucky. I'll take whatever help I can get."

She batted her lashes, and his dick shoved hard against his zipper, expecting a high-five.

"I'm eager for your expertise." She swiveled, turning her back to the bar. "What about that guy?"

For the next hour, he went through the pros and cons of every male in the building. The pros were few and far between. For good reason. He couldn't find anyone to entrust with her pleasure.

A third of them wore wedding bands. Others leered with no manners or respect. Another chunk of potentials were wiped from the board because they simply didn't look good enough.

He didn't know what it would take to earn his respect, but nobody here had even a glimpse of it, which was becoming harder to explain to Ella, who seemed to have slid on intoxication goggles and considered every man who walked through the door a potential candidate.

He'd had to point out the gay guy who only had eyes for his friend's ass.

He'd had to discuss the downfall of being with someone who spent ten minutes staring at the drink board. Because, seriously, if it took you more than two minutes to figure out your own needs, there was no point wasting a lifetime trying to determine Ella's.

The man she currently ogled wore a plaid shirt, dirty faded jeans, and muddy cowboy boots. Which, realistically, wasn't a bad thing. He looked like he had a good work ethic. But... "If you're still into fucking cattle, go for it."

She snorted, her happiness springing through him like a gunshot. "That's an unfair assumption."

He didn't give a shit.

"What about him?" She tilted her chin toward the man at the far end of the bar.

"You've gotta be kidding." The guy had stuck-up-suit written all over him.

"What's wrong with him?" she slurred through bubbles of laughter, and he immediately regretted reinstating her drinking privileges. "He's cute. He also has good fashion sense. Hell, I could ask him to strip and simply touch him for hours." She slapped her hands together in prayer. "Please, Brute, let me touch his nakedness. I can't remember the last time I got to put my hands on a guy's body."

His nostrils flared. "A few nights ago doesn't ring a bell?" Why didn't she just punch him in the dick? The injury would've hurt less than the insult.

She balked. "I barely got to touch you. Hell, girlfriend—" she waggled her head at him, "—if I had the chance to sink my nails into you, you'd know it."

"Girlfriend?" He pushed from his stool. "You're too drunk for this. Either sober up or I'll have to take you home."

She pouted. "Okay, daddy."

Fuck. Me.

She snorted again. "I'm joking. Stop glaring at me like that. Christ, you throw in a daddy line and everyone gets offended."

Yeah, he was fucking offended, because any other reaction while imagining spanking her over his knee wasn't goddamn appropriate. If only his cock would get the memo.

"I'll be back in a sec. Behave while I'm gone."

He needed a bathroom break.

An *Ella* break.

She wasn't the only one who needed to sober up. The alcohol heating his veins spewed some pretty crazy shit into his mind.

Jesus Christ, he could fucking taste her with every swallow.

Good news was, he hadn't thought of his family. Not until now, when his lust dissipated with each step.

He hadn't contemplated why his dying mother couldn't gather a glimmer of affection to call her only child to say goodbye. He hadn't pondered why his father hadn't picked up the phone—now or in the past months. He didn't think about how the two people who were supposed to love him the most hadn't given a fuck about him at all, because his concentration kept focusing back on Ella with pinpoint precision.

He shoved into the bathroom, stood in front of the basin, and stared at his reflection in the dirty mirror.

Something wasn't right.

Lust had never felt like this before. It had never started in his chest and worked its way down.

At the bar, he'd tried to convince himself it was the

alcohol, or the sob story about her husband that pulled at his usually non-existent heartstrings. This was supposed to be about Ella finding someone to fuck. It was about getting her to participate in the demonstration. It was about business. But in here, facing himself, it became harder to live the lie.

He liked her. He fucking liked her. "Damn it."

He ran his hands through his hair, entwined his fingers at the back of his head, and placed tight pressure on his skull.

This was Tera's fault. In one phone call, she'd fucked with him, messing with his head in so many ways he couldn't think straight. She'd reminded him of his childhood, and how he'd once believed in happily-ever-afters and all that naive, fairytale bullshit.

It had to stop.

He couldn't do this to himself.

He couldn't do it to Ella.

She had baggage. Issues.

The appeal didn't make sense. Yet, it was there, building from a molehill into a mountain, right before his eyes, and there was only one way to make it stop.

CHAPTER FOURTEEN

*P*amela waited until Bryan disappeared into the bathroom before she slumped against the bar and released her pent-up nervousness in an audible sigh.

This was hell. She wasn't entirely sure which of the nine circles she currently resided in—either lust or greed—but it was hell nonetheless.

Not only did she have to continue the let's-get-me-laid charade, she also had to pretend she wasn't sliding headfirst into deeper feelings for a man who'd made it clear he was off limits. She'd even stooped to the low of bringing up her late husband in the hope the tragic topic would break the early descent into puppy love.

The diversion hadn't worked in the slightest. The conversation had only achieved additional respect for a man who seemed to have more layers than puff pastry.

He'd listened to her. He'd comforted her with soft, simple words. And when the conversation became too emotional, he'd shut it down in typical Brute fashion, which made the depression instantaneously vanish.

Now, leaving wasn't an option. Being alone in a car with him was too much of a temptation to her diluted sanity.

She wanted Bryan.

She wanted Brute.

She wanted whatever she could extract from the big grizzly bear of a man and didn't care about the consequences.

"Hey, sugar."

She glanced from her empty glass to find another flannelette-wearing cowboy at her side. He was broad, tall, and tanned, with an uber smirk to boot.

"You look like you need another drink."

She gave a false smile. "I'm fine. Thanks."

He inclined his head. "That you are, but I insist." He knocked his knuckles on the bar. "Bartender, get this pretty lady a glass of bubbles."

Bubbles?

"I, um..." That went against rule five-hundred and fifty-five in the Brute's Fuck Buddy Guidebook—a potential lover should nail your drink order before he nails you.

A mini bottle of champagne cracked open before her, the contents poured into a slim flute. She should've declined with more enthusiasm. Should've, could've, would've if numbing mindlessness wasn't a mere drink away. Tomorrow, she'd pay for mixing drinks. For now, she'd take whatever relief she could get.

"Here you go." He lifted the glass from the bar and handed it over. "Something sweet for someone sweet."

She cleared her throat. "If you came here looking for timid and cute, I'm not your girl."

"You're the naughty type?" He eyed her with lust-filled appreciation. "Tonight is my lucky night."

A laugh escaped. She couldn't help it. In a game of hot and cold, this guy was so far from getting lucky he'd need a snow suit.

"I can't believe a woman as fine as yourself would be out on her own."

"She's not." Bryan came up behind her. "Take a hike, buddy."

"*Bryan*." She snapped her head around, scowling. "You don't have to be rude."

"My apologies. I didn't realize this was the type of guy you were looking for."

Was intoxication playing tricks on her, or did he seem unmistakably jealous? Her stomach flipped, and all the liquid she'd consumed went with it in a nauseating roll.

"Hold on a minute." The cowboy held up his hands. "She was sitting here on her own. I didn't know you two were together."

"We're not," they spoke in unison.

"Right." The guy retreated a step. "I guess looks can be deceiving."

Heat crept up her throat, soaking through her scarf.

"We're leaving." Bryan stared at her, demanding compliance.

Shit. He must have finally cracked the code on her not-so-subtle feelings.

"Sugar," the cowboy started. "If you're in trouble—"

"Trouble?" He thought she was in danger? From Bryan? Okay, so maybe the brute was clenching his fists and breathing heavier than normal, but that was only because she'd broken her promise not to fall for the commitment-phobic jerk. "No. I'm okay. This is what he's like. All bark. No bite."

Bryan growled. Actually growled.

"We're leaving," he repeated. "Unless you want to hang around with a guy who doesn't give you the respect of finding out what you're drinking. But, hey—" He shrugged. "—I'm sure he's a keeper. You've got great taste in men, after all."

She scoffed and downed half the champagne in one fast swallow. He itched for a fight—she could see it in the flash of anger in those deep blue eyes. She had no plan to leave him unsatisfied.

"My taste in men shouldn't be any of your business." She shoved from her stool and wobbled with the landing.

"Fucking hell." He flung out a hand to catch her.

"Don't speak to me like that." She slapped his hold away and got in his face, allowing his dark, masculine scent to mess with her senses.

"Then stop doing stupid shit."

She heard the words, and the only thing that sunk in was his protection. His authority. His claim for territory. *No.* The alcohol played tricks on her.

She stepped back and turned to Mr. Cowboy. "Sorry 'bout that." She snatched her clutch from the bar and put the champagne flute in its place. "Thanks for the drink."

The guy's eyes widened. "You're leaving with him?"

Yes. *No.* The answer didn't matter because she couldn't think without fresh air.

She hustled outside, her short, sharp toe steps making the support of her stiletto heels unpredictable.

"What the hell are you doing now?" Bryan followed, keeping a thankful yard of distance between them on the sidewalk.

"Leaving. Isn't that what you wanted?"

His fury tickled the back of her neck in the form of a snarl. She hated that noise. Hated it so much her pussy contracted and released enough times to mimic an orgasm.

"When it comes to you, I get nothing I want."

His retort hit her like a slap across the face. She swung around, teetering again, her heels producing the same stability as cooked spaghetti. "Then what *do* you want, Bryan? Tell me."

He crossed his arms over his broad chest, making his jacket gape and the material of his shirt temptingly tighten over the muscles beneath.

Oh, dear God.

The entire world conspired against her attempts to dislike him. Every time she erected blocks to combat the attraction, he'd shove them down again in one mighty Hulk smash.

"I want you to fucking listen." His breath came in exhausting huffs. "I'm trying to show you how to find a guy who deserves you. Someone who's going to give a shit about what you want. And the minute I turn my back you're hooking up with Cowboy Bill."

"Hooking up?" *Hooking up*? "He offered to buy me a drink. I declined. And he didn't take no for an answer. I didn't even take a sip of the champagne until you came back and inspired the need for alcoholism."

He glared, those blue irises harsh with menace.

"Come on." She sighed. "What's this really about?"

"You know what this is about." The words grated through perfect teeth, across lush, smooth lips.

She wanted to nod and confirm that, yes, this was about feelings neither one of them could ignore. This was about something more than friendship or sex or the Vault. This was about sparks and connection and heart-clenching emotion.

"This is about needing a demonstration assistant," he snarled. "That's all this has ever been."

Her nose tingled, throat pinched. "I know that." But she hadn't. Not really. She'd tried to forget. She'd ignored the entire purpose of them being together while becoming overrun with the allure of romance.

Again.

This was Lucas on repeat.

"Good," he snapped.

"*Great*," she mimicked.

154

He approached, getting in her face. His nostrils flared, his lip curled. "*Fucking* perfect."

She'd never wanted to kiss him more. The thrill of having his beard scratch against her mouth, her neck, her breasts. Her heart thundered. Her throat pinched tighter. She whirled on her toes and escaped in the opposite direction, the *click*, *click*, *click* of her heels a panicked staccato.

"God, I wish I knew why you were such a grumpy jerk." She approached the edge of the building and turned into the darkened parking lot, remaining close to the brickwork in case she needed the support.

"Slow down. You're going to wind up on your ass."

"Stop it, okay?" She glared over her shoulder. "Stop the back and forth. The Jekyll and Hyde. The kindness and severity. I'm sick of it." Her ankle rolled, the sharp twinge of pain shooting up the outside of her leg. She tilted, the threat of falling on her butt replaced with something even more threatening—his hold.

He grabbed her, tugging her against his strong chest and lunging her into the brickwork. She was boxed in, caught between two layers of cold sterility. But that wasn't what stared back at her. Those blue eyes weren't barren. She could see everything peering down at her—his affection, his lust, his hopes for the future. Then, in a blink, they disappeared.

"Jesus Christ." He held her upright, keeping her caged. "I never should've brought you here."

Regret took over his expression. Annoyance, too. Her delusional fairytale of what they'd shared became tarnished by the frustration staring down at her.

"I'm sorry."

His brows pulled tight. "Why?"

"I don't know." A breath shuddered from her lungs. "I feel like I need to apologize. I've never offended anyone as much as I seem to offend you." She had to keep talking, if only to make sure he remained nestled against her, his warmth finally sinking in. They'd never been this close. Not emotionally. "I guess I lost sight of this being about your job. I began to think we were friends."

His body relaxed.

No, it deflated. His shoulders slumped, his face fell. "You don't offend me, Ella."

"Then what is it?" she whispered.

He turned his head away, the tension building in his frame until he loomed over her as he focused on the street.

"Bryan?" She reached out, her fingertips tingling the closer she came to his beard-covered cheek. Her palm slid over the coarse hairs, and everything inside her crumpled. She'd never touched him. Not like this. Not with her heart in her throat and her feelings exposed in the brief connection.

She guided his face back to hers and pleaded with her eyes. "What's this all about?"

The hardness of his jaw became more defined. "It's about wanting to fuck you. I've gone insane for the last five hours, fighting the need to get you under me. And the five days before that." He stepped forward, squeezing her tighter between the hard wall of the building and the harder wall of his chest. "Even before that, Ella. Since the first night I touched you in the fucking locker room."

Hope took the reins and ran. Everything inside her ignited, emotions and body parts all combusting to cause a mass of burning, tingling flesh.

She had to kiss him. Had to taste those lips and feel them devastating hers. And that was exactly what they'd do— devastate her. Destroy her. Because one passionate kiss would be so much more than she'd had from her husband.

He rocked into her, the solid length of his shaft making itself known against her pubic bone. She couldn't breathe.

Couldn't think. All she could do was become ensnared as his mouth called her name like a siren's song.

She smashed her lips to his and immediately drowned in the intensity of his reciprocation. His hand flew to her hair, sliding over her scalp, holding her close. His arm wrapped around her waist, squeezing life back into her. Every part of him touched her. Every inch of her body remained at his mercy, while his tongue parted her lips and delved deep.

He took over. Made her hyperventilate. All with one kiss.

With only his beard, lips, and teeth.

When he pulled back, they both panted into the small space between them. "We should get out of here."

She nodded.

His hand left her hair, snaked down her arm, and entwined with her fingers. He didn't acknowledge the intimacy, didn't even look her in the eye anymore. Instead, he turned and led her to the car, not stopping until they stood at the passenger door, his free hand poised on the handle.

He remained close, frozen against her, as if the world had stopped for them to have this moment. At least that was how it felt, until comprehension dawned.

"You can't drive, can you?"

He released her hand and wiped a rough palm over his mouth. "I've had too much to drink."

He remained pressed against her, the teasing torment of her feelings flickering between them like rapidly igniting sparks. She tried to think of a sensible way out of this situation. Something that wouldn't leave her broken tomorrow. But want and need fried those rational thoughts, leaving her alone with the chemical imbalance driving her to clutch his shirt and pull him closer.

"Do you want to catch a cab?" She lifted her clutch over her shoulder and placed it on the roof of his car.

A lifetime of racing heartbeats measured the seconds they

remained close, the intoxication rapidly leaving her system in a passion-induced detox.

"You know I don't." His touch returned to her hip. "Not yet."

The pulse of his dick nestled against her. The thickness, the length, made her salivate. She couldn't budge. It wasn't the inescapable cage of his arms. It was his nearness. His proximity. The promise of more.

"Are you sure you want to do this now?" he asked, his breath drifting over her cheek, inspiring exhilaration, goose bumps, and nausea in overlapping doses.

She was entirely wrecked by this man.

"Are you sure you want to finish this here?" He nuzzled into her hair, his nose teasing her neck, his beard scratching her skin. He gripped her chin, guiding her gaze to his penetrating eyes while his thigh parted hers, his weight pinning her to the car.

"Yes." The word was a breathy exhale. "Here. Now."

He ground into her, tearing a whimper from her throat. He was already so close to fucking her, a mere unbuckle of his belt and the raise of her dress. She could sense how cataclysmic the penetration would be. How perfect. But... "I'm scared this isn't going to end well."

She needed his reassurance. Craved it as much as she craved his cock.

"Doesn't matter. We both know this is inevitable," he countered, gripping her dress.

She couldn't stop him. There was no will. Her body gave her no choice.

All she could do was stare into that fierce face as he focused on her with pure ownership and lifted her hem. Inch by inch, the tight material crawled up her body, exposing her flesh with agonizing lethargy. The cool night air seeped into her thighs, her hips, her sex. And still, those eyes pinned her, reading the reactions she tried to hide.

He released the fabric to bundle at her waist, then slid his hands down her bare skin, searing the flesh he touched.

"You weren't lying about not wearing underwear."

"I have no reason to lie to you." She could've laughed at the hypocrisy. She'd been lying to him all night. This afternoon, too. She'd lied about her feelings. About her intent. She'd lied and lied and lied. Even to herself. "This dress doesn't look anywhere near as sexy with visible panty lines." She lied again. The lack of underwear had been to tease him. To see if he was affected by her the way she was by him.

"Well..." He grinned. "I've never appreciated honesty more than I do right now." He gripped her chin, demanding her attention. A gentle fingertip glided over her tingling lower lip, the connection more painful and emotional than anything she could've expected.

Her insides waged war. Half of her screamed to take all she could get. The other ached to tell him what another kiss would mean. To make him understand. Even though nobody else ever had. Not even her mother or Kim.

This time when he leaned in, she held her breath, waiting for his next move. Those tempting lips approached, only to veer at the last second and plague her cheek with the burn. "I could've sworn you weren't the type to fuck in a parking lot," he whispered against her skin. "But you have a habit of surprising me."

His beard grazed each place of impact, along her jaw, then further, to the sensitive spot below her ear. She wanted to hate the misplaced sentiment. Wanted to hate him in general. But those light kisses turned into nibbles, the nibbles transforming into bites and sucks, until he ravaged her neck with such erotic efficiency she clung to his shoulders for more.

"Take off the scarf." He ground into her, his erection thick and pulsing between them.

"If I take it off, are you going to leave more marks?"

"Without a doubt."

Oh, God. She couldn't have asked for a better response.

She slid the silk from her neck. The delicate glide inspired goose bumps. Her skin erupted in a mass of tingles. She held the material out to him and pretended it didn't affect her when he placed his hand over hers, stealing the scarf from her grip.

"Now, open your mouth."

She recoiled. "Excuse me?"

"Trust me, you're going to want something in that mouth to stop you crying out."

"I'll be quiet."

"Really?" The silk fell to his side while his free hand skimmed the trim patch of curls at the apex of her thighs. With a quick slide of his fingers, he grazed her clit and parted her folds, teasing her slit. She moaned with the sharp infusion of pleasure. The noise was long, low and entirely out of control.

"Do you want to rethink that promise?" He pulsed the tip of two fingers at her entrance, eyeing her with confidence while he worked his magic.

Her chest exploded, the shrapnel shooting to her breasts, her abdomen, her core.

"How do you think you're going to react once I slide my cock in here?"

He raised the scarf and a confident brow at the same time.

Damn him. For everything.

"Fine." She jutted her chin, waiting.

His eyes blazed as he removed his fingers from between her legs to place the material in her mouth. She bit down while he crossed it behind her neck, then guided it forward to hang over her chest.

"Now give me your wrists."

She shook her head, working the material from her mouth. "No."

"Don't trust me?

"No. I don't. Not out here. Not when I'm already vulnerable enough."

A flash of rejection marred his features. "I wouldn't hurt you, Ella. Not like that."

Not. Like. That.

Just in every other way imaginable.

He worked the silk between her lips and tightened the knot behind her neck. "There. Pretty as a picture and even more inviting now that you can't talk."

"You're a piece of work, you know that?" The words were mumbled into utter incoherence.

"What was that?"

"Fuck you."

He smirked. "You'll be doing that soon enough."

A hand glided between them, those talented fingers rediscovering her entrance, spreading her folds. This time, her accompanying whimper barely sounded, smothered by delicate material.

"That's better." He bent forward. "Now I won't have to hold back."

She would've hated if he had. She couldn't wait to see his mindlessness. His restraint and subsequent surrender.

"I love how you're always wet for me. Are you like this for everyone?"

She shook her head. *No.* Nobody but him.

"Good." He trailed two fingers around in circles, not

stopping the motion as he retrieved a wallet from his back pocket, flipped the leather open, and rested it against his hip to pull a condom from the notes section. Once he had what he wanted, he dropped the wallet to the ground, his cards, coins, and notes scattering across the asphalt.

He didn't seem to notice. Didn't seem to care.

He placed the condom packet between his teeth and unbuckled his belt one-handed. The *clink, clink, clink* of metal on metal broke the quiet night air, followed by the grate of his zipper. She watched, her breath catching as he shoved at his waistband and fisted his erect length in his palm.

She was really doing this. Really shoving herself into a situation that could only end in heartbreak. *Again.*

But who cared?

She'd recovered before.

She reached out, trailing her nails along his shaft, then gripped the base with a tight squeeze.

"Fuck." The curse was guttural, defenseless, and entirely perfect.

Behind the scarf, she smiled.

He released his dick and spat the condom packet into his palm. "So, you want me to blow in your hand, is that it?" He closed his eyes and dropped his head back. The worst part was his fingers sliding from between her thighs. "Come on, sweetheart. You need to let me suit up. Neither one of us want to see me finish like this."

Maybe she did.

Maybe it was best for them both.

He was under her control, susceptible to her touch, just like she was to his. The knowledge made her attraction all the more punishing. He was so beautiful, his face a mix of tension and control as moonlight beamed down on those harsh features.

"*Ella.*" The way he said her nickname—the plea, the

passion, the lust. "This isn't what you want... You need my hands on your ass... My mouth on your neck... My cock in your pussy."

Her lips burned with dryness she couldn't lick away. All she could do was bite down on silk and whimper.

"You've got five seconds," he murmured. "Four..."

She trailed her touch to the head of his shaft and rubbed the moisture beading at his slit.

"I lied." He gripped her wrist and dragged her hand away. "You're done." His other arm snaked behind her back, lifting her off the ground. "Legs around my waist."

She complied without thought, her ass sliding against the side of the car, his dick poised at her entrance as he worked the protection over his length in efficient strokes.

All too soon, he was ready and looking at her as if asking permission.

"Do it," she mumbled around the gag. "Just do it."

His jaw clenched. "You sure?"

Goddamn him and his sweet concern.

She threw her hands around his neck and sank her nails deep. If those scars weren't enough to convince him to hurry, the buck of her hips should've been.

He slid his hand to the top of his shaft, working the tip back and forth along her entrance. She didn't know where to train her gaze—on his impressive cock, his muscled chest, or those penetrating eyes now framed by strands of loose hair.

He blinked at her, sweat beading his brow as he snaked his tongue out to moisten his gorgeous lips. She became lost in the moment. Lost in him.

He thrust home in one long, punishing shove of his hips, stealing all the breath from her lungs. All the thoughts from her mind. There was only friction. Only pleasure.

She cried out, her head falling back, her fingers clenching tight into his neck. The heat of him enveloped her chest, the weight pressing deep. His hips rocked in a slow, torturous rhythm and she whimpered with each undulation, the sound ringing louder and louder in her ears.

"Hey." He placed his mouth a breath away from hers. "Keep it quiet, sweetheart. You're not going to find a friendly audience in this shoddy neighborhood."

Her breathing quickened with her jerky nod and she bit around the silk to sink her teeth into her lower lip. She wiggled, trying to seat her ass on the edge of the window and slipped.

"It's okay." He gripped her tight. "I've got you."

Did he? Really?

Physically, he was there. But emotionally, she wasn't sure he existed.

"Fuck." He thrust. Again and again. Each pleasure-induced pulse followed with a panted breath against her lips. "What are you doing to me?"

She closed her eyes, wishing she could close her ears, too, because his words were sinking into her soul, never to be removed. *So damn good... Drive me crazy... Fuck... Best damn thing...*She wanted to scream for him to stop and beg for this to never end.

He kissed her neck, her shoulder, then the deep V of her dress, marking the curves of her breasts with lips and tongue and beard. She'd never been more alive. More hopeful. She wanted to share the world with this man and believed he craved the same thing. Maybe not on the surface, but deep down. Deep, deep down. Almost within reach.

"I want to do everything to you." He thrust hard. Over and over, each undulation growing in force.

"Yes." She gasped around her gag. "More."

She was close, already. He had a way of knowing her. Of sensing where to touch. Where to focus.

He grazed her nipples through her dress. The first time

was too light, the second too hard. The third and every time after was utter perfection. He was Goldilocks. Testing everything. Finding the right fit. He even had the hair to prove it.

"What are you smiling at?" His nose brushed hers.

She couldn't explain, even if she was physically able.

"I love your smile." He nuzzled her cheek, his beard leaving its mark. "Prettiest damn thing I've ever seen."

Her grin vanished, pure shock taking its place. *Oh, God.* Her heart stopped. It didn't start again—just remained idle as his mouth trekked her mouth, finally coming to rest on the corner of her lips.

"What?" He pulled back. "What is it? Have I done something wrong?"

He kept compounding her awe. Kept showing a side of himself even more alluring than what she'd already fallen for.

He froze, those sexy undulations ceasing to exist. "Ella?"

She worked the scarf from her mouth, no longer caring if she drew a crowd because she couldn't go a moment longer without his kiss. "You've done everything right."

She shoved a hand through his hair and dragged his face to hers, stealing his lips. Their connection ignited, the mix of tongues and teeth and renewed thrusts building to a crazy intensity that had every inch of her in love with every inch of him.

He kissed her as hard as his cock fucked her. He worshipped her just as sweetly, too. His touch was a fine contrast to all the slamming body parts.

"You're going to make me come." She spoke into his mouth, pulling his hair.

"I fucking hope so."

Her pussy contracted around his length, tiny spasms quickly building to impending bliss. "Bryan..."

"I got you."

He did. He really did.

She came undone, the whimpered noises building in her throat, only to be smothered by his mouth. He continued to kiss her. To love her like nobody had ever loved her.

"*Shit*." His fingers dug into her ass, marking flesh she never wanted to heal. He pistoned his hips, extending her orgasm as he came, thrust after torturous thrust.

He bit and sucked and licked. Bucked and caressed and squeezed.

Her world became one mass of tingling sensation. Then just as quickly, it faded.

Starbursts turned into twinkles. Pulses lessened to twinges. She pulled back, panting into the night air while his rhythm lessened to a slow dance.

She slumped against his shoulder, his scent filling her lungs, his sweat coating her cheek.

One moment, bliss conquered. The next, the hard weight of reality made her numb. She hadn't merely fallen a few steps for this man—she'd toppled down a slope the size of Everest.

"Ella," he whispered into her neck, a hint of regret tinging his voice.

She closed her eyes, not wanting to know the harshness inevitably due to follow all the sexy sweetness she'd received. "Mmm?"

"I'm sorry this had to end."

Her heart swelled as she worked the tight silk from around her neck. "*Had to* end? What do you mean?"

He spoke in past tense, like this was already over. As if it had been a foregone conclusion that they would share a monumentally deep connection, then wave each other goodbye.

He settled her on her feet and stepped back, frowning. "You knew this was the end, right?"

Her eyes seared, threatening to betray her.

"Ella?" His voice turned into a warning. "You knew this game was over once we fucked."

She blinked and blinked, trying to hide her cluelessness while he righted his clothing.

"I told you from the start. I tell *everyone* from the start."

"Yeah." She swallowed. Licked her lips. "I knew. I just..." She tugged down the hem of her dress and snatched her clutch from the top of the car. "I didn't—" She clamped her mouth shut and inched away, taking close, cautious steps.

"Wait." He reached out and the connection of his hand missed its mark. "I thought you understood. You spoke about this not ending well. I made sure you wanted to finish this *here. Now.* I asked you, Ella. I thought we were both on the same page."

She hadn't even been in the same book.

She'd momentarily forgotten his rules and regulations, too blinded by the dreamy thoughts of what could be. She'd made herself believe that something special was a possibility. Just like she had with Lucas.

"We were," she lied with a jerky nod. "We *are*."

"Then why are you looking at me like..."

Don't say it. Please don't say it.

"Why are you backing away from me?" he amended.

"Because that's what you want." She stopped, commanding her feet to remain in place even though she itched to kick off her heels and sprint. "I'm giving you space. I know how much you hate clingy women."

He winced, and for the briefest second she expected him to tell her to come back into his arms.

Yet again, she was wrong.

Why did she keep getting this so wrong? She pinned her hopes on love when it was nowhere in sight. She continued to fall for men who had no intention of falling for her.

"Did you expect this to turn into something more?" His

jaw tensed as his hands stabbed through his hair. "I can't fucking read you."

"*No*," she lied and scrambled to come up with solid reasoning. "I just didn't think you'd be fucking me one minute and kicking me to the curb the next." She backtracked, each step bringing more necessary space. "But I get it. You made your position clear. And I certainly don't want to be classified as one of your groupies."

"*Fuck*." His curse rang through every inch of the parking lot, startling her. "Just stop." His hands fell to his sides. "I don't want you to be pissed at me."

"Why does it matter?" Her question held too much heartache, the weakness ringing in her ears. "You know I want to cancel my Vault membership. After tonight, you'll never see me again. So, who gives a shit if I'm pissed?"

He clenched his teeth. "I do, okay? I want you back at the club. I want to help you find someone."

"No, thank you." Not when she wanted that someone to be him. "Your help tonight was enough."

He stepped toward her and froze when the crunch of plastic sounded under his sole. "*Shit*." He crouched to pick up his wallet and the scattered credit cards. "Look, Ella, I've got a truckload of bullshit on my shoulders. My family is fucked. The guys at work are on my back about the argument we had at the club..."

"And the last thing you need is what? Me causing you problems?" When had she become a liability instead of an asset for his demonstration?

His lips parted, but an answer hovered out of reach. *Everything* hovered out of reach. If only she had the heart to stretch a little further. To find the perfect words to make him realize. To do something, anything, to make him wake up and see the possibilities right in front of him.

"You're a great guy, Bryan," she whispered. "But I deserve better than this."

He scoffed, his hand paused on a dirty business card, his hair framing his gorgeous face. He didn't look at her. Didn't move. "Ain't that the truth." His voice was barely audible, the softness far more punishing than if he'd growled at her.

He sat back on his haunches, those brilliant eyes hitting her with feigned sincerity. "What a fucking mess, right?"

She slowly nodded through the disbelief. "Yeah..."

What else could she say? She wasn't going to stand here and argue with him while her heart slowly bled out. "I'm going to catch a cab." A chill took over her skin, sinking deeper to penetrate bone. She wanted to hate him and couldn't. Wanted to stop adoring him and failed at that, too.

"Wait." He rushed to pick up more of his scattered belongings. "Let me get all this shit first and we can leave together." He snatched at the coins, notes, and credit cards strewn across the asphalt. "Give me a second."

"No. You want this to end now. At least let me have the dignity of walking away."

"You can, *after* I get you home safely."

The concern was a weighty sucker-punch. He cared about her, but not enough to ditch his stupid rules. "I've been single a long time. I'm sure I'll be fine on my own."

"*Ella.*"

The word tore her apart—her skin, her ribs, her heart. She gave him one last look, taking in all the severity framed by pure gorgeousness and turned on her heels. "I've told you before, that's not my name."

CHAPTER FIFTEEN

*B*ryan kept his attention on his computer as Shay came to stand inside the doorway of the Shot of Sin office. Her presence was never a good thing. Not lately, anyway.

"We're ready for the management meeting. When are you coming down?"

"I'm skipping it." He didn't raise his focus. "Take notes for me."

"You already missed last week's meeting. And the one before that."

He slid his palm over the pen laying on the table, his fingers clutching the flimsy plastic in a death grip. "And if I want, I'll miss the next one, too. You know you don't need me to participate."

"Brute..." She approached his desk.

"*Shay*, I'm not in the mood."

"You know they're only going to bring the meeting up here if you don't get your ass downstairs."

His friends must have reached the threshold of his bullshit. About time, too. He'd expected them to cave more than a week ago, and he still hadn't been able to pull himself out of the spiral of bad behavior.

"Was that your brilliant idea?" He pinched the bridge of his nose, already knowing the answer.

"You know I'm always trying to figure out how to get more Brute time."

He sighed and rested back in the chair. He'd been ignoring everyone for weeks, successfully keeping enough distance to avoid their nagging eyes. "I'll be down there in a minute."

"Good." She boasted her victory with a slight quirk of her lips. "You still doing okay?"

"Why wouldn't I be?"

"Do you really want me to spell it out?"

"What I want is for you to get the fuck out of my office." And for Ella to get out of his mind. It seemed he was destined to give a shit about women who didn't give a shit about him. First his mother, then the sexual goddess in the Vault who had his gray matter running a minefield of pathetic emotions.

"I will, as soon as you follow me downstairs." She smiled, big and broad, and backtracked toward the door. "Come on."

"I said I'll be down in a minute."

He needed to pull his shit together before the inevitable slew of questions. He'd left everyone in the lurch for almost three weeks without explanation or remorse over why he'd bunkered down in the office, demanding to be the reclusive office bitch.

He'd played Tetris with the once-perfect work roster, moving employees around like puzzle pieces to fill the holes his absence made. All he could handle were emails, stock orders, and bookwork. Everything else had been left to T.J. and Leo, along with a disgruntled team of staff who'd never liked him anyway.

Most of the time he sat staring at his phone, waiting for calls that never came. One from Tampa. The other from Ella.

Neither connection seemed likely to happen, and each day of radio silence made him more annoyed. At himself. He should've known better, on both counts, than to expect a different outcome.

But he'd still texted Ella days after their night in the parking lot. It hadn't been much in the way of communication. A few sentences to encourage a conversation that never eventuated—*I gave your books to a local oncologist. He appreciated your donation and said he'd pass them on to interested patients.*

He couldn't blame her for cutting him off. That was what he'd set out to achieve when he slept with her. *That*, and to get her as far away from the dick at the bar who couldn't spare five seconds to ask what she wanted to drink.

She deserved better.

Truth be told, she deserved better than someone who would call her out in the middle of a sex club. Or fuck her in a dark parking lot in a shitty neighborhood. Or let her catch a cab home on her own after she'd been drinking.

He was no better than the champagne-buying prick.

And her lack of reply was a good indication she knew it, too.

"What's going on with you, Brute?"

"*Shit*." He startled at Shay's voice. "Why are you still lurking?"

She cocked her head and scrutinized every inch of his face. "Something really bad is up with you, isn't it?"

"Apart from my annoyance levels from your constant nagging, no." The cloying thoughts of going back to Tampa didn't help. He'd contemplated making the trip every damn day. There was a hatchet to bury, if only for his sake, because his parents made it clear they still wished he'd been swallowed instead of conceived.

But it was about closure, right?

Or something similar. He'd read a convoluted online article outlining paragraphs of psychological drivel stating all the reasons to be the better person. All of which made a lot of sense. Just not enough to convince him to pack his bags.

Not yet, at least.

"You sure? You haven't been brutish lately. I was thinking of changing your nickname to melon."

He scowled.

"Because you're so melancholy," she explained.

He pushed all the air from his lungs. Before Ella, Shay's taunting had kept him on his toes. She was an annoyance he enjoyed reciprocating. Now, all he wanted to do was sink his head back against the chair and go to sleep. "Get out, Shay."

"See, that right there is a stellar indication of your melon state. Brute would've told me to try it and see how I liked the unemployment line, but this melon uses a defeated tone to tell me to leave."

"I don't have time for this."

Her expression stilled as she contemplated him, then slowly her face fell and a potent look of concern bore down on him. "Now I'm really starting to worry."

"Look, I'm fine, okay? I've got shit going on. Personal shit. But it's nothing I can't handle."

"You know you can talk to me if you need someone."

He glared. "Seriously?"

"Don't be like that. We're friends. I care about you."

He closed his eyes and massaged his lids. "I'm not the talking type. You know that." At least he hadn't been. Not until Ella. That woman seemed to bring out the verbal diarrhea in him. She currently knew more about his life than his closest friends.

"Well, maybe you should be. It wouldn't kill you."

"It might."

She chuckled, the sound half-hearted. "Have it your way. But just so you know, if you're not downstairs in five minutes, I'm bringing the team up here."

"Yeah, I heard."

Her footsteps faded down the hall, allowing the shit running through his head to reassemble and gain traction. This whole situation had started because Shay had wanted him to help a random chick obtain an orgasm.

But Ella hadn't turned out to be a random chick, and what he'd given her hadn't merely been an orgasm. She'd taken much more from him. Too much more. And he had no idea how to get those parts of himself back.

He was stuck feeling too hollow and too heavy, at the same time. There was darkness, as well as picture-perfect clarity. Unpredictability and painful routine.

He pushed from his chair and made his way downstairs to fast-track the punishment. There was no point holding out any longer. His friends had been patient, far more than he would've been in return.

They all sat in a line, positioned across the stools at the main Shot bar. Leo, Shay, Cassie, and T.J.—all of them holding matching blank expressions as he walked behind the bar to face them head on.

"You're late." Leo slid a stack of mail across the counter. "And you might want to consider checking the mail every once in a while if you plan to continue being the office bitch. This must've been sitting in our box for weeks."

"It was on my to-do list." He grasped the envelopes and flicked through the pile, finding a mass of potential bills and one hand-written address.

"You seem like you've been busy in the office." T.J.'s statement sounded like more of a question.

"How are you handling the detox from the Vault?" Cassie asked.

"It's a piece of cake." It wasn't a lie. He hadn't stepped foot inside the sex club in weeks and had no interest in going down there in the near future. Not until he got his head sorted out. His dick, too.

"Speaking of to-do lists." Leo cleared his throat. "Did you refund everyone's money for the demonstration night?"

The reminder made him tense. "It's done." He ripped open the first envelope and retrieved the folded invoice inside before discarding the rubbish onto the counter. "I've refunded everyone involved."

"Did you explain the cancellation?"

"It's nobody's business."

"Not even ours?" Leo stared him down. "What happened, Brute? We've handled you with kid gloves for weeks, but now it's time for an explanation. I thought you were determined not to let the women win."

"They didn't win. I needed a break from the Vault." Not only the setting, the carnality, and the people. He needed a break from the reminder of what had driven him into this mind fuck. "And Ella couldn't participate either. So, the cancellation worked for both of us."

"Did you refund her membership?" T.J. asked. "It would be a nice gesture of goodwill."

His hand paused in the middle of tearing open the second envelope. "I'm not kicking her out of the club. She can return whenever she wants."

"She's not coming back," Cassie spoke softly.

He continued to open the envelope, his gaze focused on the shredding paper. A tight restriction took place behind his sternum, the pain intensifying with the need for answers to questions he didn't want to voice. Tighter and tighter his lungs squeezed, until he couldn't hold it in anymore. "You've spoken to her?"

"I called her," Shay answered.

He emptied the invoice from the envelope, threw the rubbish to the counter, and then started the process all over again. "I didn't realize the two of you were friends."

"We're not. Not really. But I wanted to check on her."

"How'd you get her number?" He couldn't hide the pathetic jealousy in his voice.

"I looked in the Vault database."

His foot to tapped against the polished floorboards, the rampant beat out of his control. "You were on my computer?"

"She was on *our* computer," T.J. corrected.

"Right." He slashed another envelope and turned back to Shay. "And she said she isn't coming back?"

The nod and accompanying look of pity were enough to send his fingers tearing through the paper.

"Did she say why?" He already knew her original reason—nobody interested her in the Vault. But he'd hoped her mind would change with time.

"Are you asking because you hope we don't know the answer?" Cassie rested her elbows on the bar, leaning forward, fully invested. "Or do you truly not know?"

He shredded another envelope and kept his mouth shut, not wanting to admit he was to blame. He didn't need to exacerbate his pathetic existence.

Shay sighed.

Leo crossed his arms over his chest.

Cassie glanced at T.J., while her husband pinned him with a sympathetic stare.

He opened three envelopes in quick succession and pulled out the accompanying information. "What's next on the agenda?"

Uncomfortable silence fell until T.J. had the balls to fill it.

"We still haven't resolved the current topic. Are you able to refund her membership? Maybe write a check and put it in the mail?"

Another envelope died in his hands, the front half ripping in two. He didn't want to think about her any more than he already did. He didn't want to look up her details on his computer. Or scribble her name on a check. But taking this route and getting his friends off his back was the lesser of two evils. "Yeah. No problem. I'll sort it out."

"Great. We can move on, then." Cassie gave her co-conspirators a warning look, wordlessly reiterating how pathetic and temperamental he was. "Next on the list is the possibility of an under-age dance night."

That was his cue to zone out of the conversation. His field of fucks was well and truly barren. Everything felt raw and uncomfortable. Even answering the simplest of questions. All because of Ella—a woman who hadn't called and evidently had no plans to see him again.

She'd forgotten him.

And with all his determination and focus, he still couldn't seem to do the same with her.

Turned out, his insurance policy was a piece of shit.

He tore open the last envelope, this time slower, drawing out the need to keep his hands occupied. There were no folded pages this time. He parted the opening and sank his hand in to retrieve the tiny slip of paper buried inside.

A newspaper clipping.

He read the heading and wondered if he'd fallen into a momentary hallucination. He blinked, blinked again, and re-read the words. He stared for long moments, his chest tightening, bile rising in his throat.

"Brute?" Shay's voice was distant. A million miles away.

"*Bryan?*" Cassie pleaded. "What is it?"

He slid the paper back into the envelope and ran a hand

over his beard, hoping to encourage his lunch to stay in his gut. "Nothing." His response was static. "Can you finish up without me? I need to sort out this mail and get started on the refund for Ella."

Ella. *Fucking Ella*. At a time like this, she was still at the forefront of his mind.

Pinched brows aimed at him. Worried eyes, too.

"What's going on?" Leo glanced at the envelopes in Bryan's hand. "Is there something in the mail I need to know about?"

"No." He was on his own with this. Like he always had been. Like he'd always wanted to be. He never should've contemplated a deviation. "I'll fill you in later if anything becomes important."

He made for the upstairs staircase. Once he was out of view, he ran, taking the steps two at a time, pounding out the motions until he was behind the closed door of the office and leaning against the hard wood.

He was done. So fucking done with life and work and people.

The mail crunched in his closing fist as devastation seared a scorching trail through his veins. Every inch of him was out of control—his mind, his pulse, his tingling limbs.

He'd never needed something more than he did right now. And for the life of him, he didn't know what that something was. He only knew there was a hole in his chest. A massive, gaping crater, screaming to be filled.

He couldn't breathe through it. Couldn't think around the pain of it. Everything was closing in—his mistakes, his insecurities. Every little thing he hated about his existence bore down on him with enough force to crush him.

Nothing gave him hope.

Not. One. Thing.

All he had was the dizzying punishment of all the mistakes he'd made.

He rushed toward the desk, grabbed a fresh envelope from the drawer and scrawled *Pamela* across the front. Those six letters were a death sentence.

No. They'd been a life sentence. Years upon years of unwanted sterile independence.

He transferred the newspaper clipping into the unripped envelope, making sure not to read the words demanding his attention, then encapsulated the information by sealing the back. He stood staring at the name, hating it, his anger building, growing.

He tore his attention away and scoured the perfect alignment on the desk. The pens, Post-Its, and stationery items all had their own place, their own function in the world. While he remained in limbo, stuck thinking about what he was good for.

In one harsh swipe of his arm he sent everything flying, the symmetry transforming into a scattered mess on the floor. The destruction brought relief, the tiniest flicker of havoc sating his self-loathing.

He did it again, this time pulling the drawer from the desk and throwing it across the room. And again, with the second drawer. And again, with the filing trays.

His blood raced with dizzying speed, the lightheaded delirium righting some of his wrongs.

Most, but not all.

Ella still stared back at him from his mind. Taunting him. Reminding him of his biggest mistake. He never should've touched her. Never should've given a shit. Because now she was stuck in his head. Unable to get out.

All he wanted was for her to get out.

To leave him alone.

To stop torturing him with the one thing he wanted but nobody could ever give him.

"*Fuck.*" His shout echoed off the walls.

He had to find a way out of this. To make his head stop pounding. He spun around, his gaze catching on the bookshelf, the parallel lines of immaculate book spines taunting him with their equilibrium.

"Fuck you," he spat.

Fuck their easy existence and harmonious balance.

Fuck their effortlessness and their calm.

Fuck everything and everyone, because he couldn't take it anymore.

Breaths heaved from his lungs. His limbs ached. His forehead heated with sweat.

"*Fuck. You.*" He stormed toward the bookshelf and gripped the heavy wood in his hands. Then in one effortless pull, he created more destruction.

CHAPTER SIXTEEN

*P*amela raised her gaze to the person walking into the deserted cafe. "What can I get—" The words died on her lips, the familiar face bringing memories she eagerly tried to bury.

"Hi, Pamela." The blonde gave a half-hearted smile as she clutched a large wicker basket in her hand. "I'm Cassie from Shot of Sin."

"I know. We've met before." The woman was T.J.'s wife and a regular participant at the Vault.

"Sometimes we're not easily recognizable with our clothes on." The faux tilt of her lips increased.

"I suppose so." Pamela grabbed the portafilter from the coffee machine and dumped the used puck into the refuse chute. "What can I get for you?"

"Actually, I've got something for you." Cassie raised the basket and placed it on the counter. "This is yours."

"Why?" She paused the cleaning routine and scoped the contents of the basket from the corner of her eye. Inside lay an array of different items. Two bottles of wine. Chips. Bar nuts. A small bottle of vodka. Along with other things hidden beneath.

"I hoped you might be able to tell me the answer to that. Bryan asked me to deliver it to you."

"Bryan?" She raised a disbelieving brow. "He asked you to deliver me a basket of goodies?" The same Bryan who had been nicknamed for his brutality? The same Bryan who told her their time together was over? "Sorry. I think you've got the wrong person."

The woman broke eye contact.

"Why are you really here, Cassie?" She shoved the portafilter back into the machine and slid along the counter, meeting the woman face to face. "We both know he didn't send you here."

There was a beat of silence while T.J.'s wife turned a bright shade of pink. "Wow." She gave an awkward chuckle. "I thought this would've played out a little longer than five seconds."

"Bryan playing Santa is as far-fetched as it gets." Pamela struggled to keep her tone friendly.

"I guess. I just thought things between the two of you may have been different."

It was Pamela's turn to crumple under the burn of reddening cheeks. "Nope. You're wrong there, too." She glanced away, meeting Kim's gaze as she strode from the kitchen. "Bryan has no need to get back in contact with me."

"That's not entirely true." Cassie reached into the basket and pulled out a pristine envelope. "He wanted you to have this."

"I'm sorry, I don't bel—"

"Look, it even has your name on it. It's a refund for your membership. He wanted to make sure you were reimbursed."

Pamela crossed her arms over her chest, determined not to buy what she was selling, even though her heart wanted to.

The only communication she'd had from Bryan was a lone, emotionless text. He hadn't mentioned what they'd shared or how he felt. He'd only spoken about her books. The damn cancer reminders.

"I promise he wanted you to have this." Cassie handed it over. "He just may have planned to mail it to you. That's all. The basket was an excuse for me to see you."

"And why would you want to do that?" She ignored the offering as Kim came up beside her, hovering close.

Cassie eyed them both, appearing more fragile than deceptive. "Have you got time to talk?"

"Not really. I'm working." She ignored the empty cafe and the fact it was less than thirty minutes from closing.

"*Please.*" It wasn't a request. It was a plea. "It's important."

"Hear her out." Kim nudged her elbow. "You're not going to sleep tonight if you send her away. Listen to what she has to say, and we'll deal with it from there."

"It won't take long," Cassie added.

Pamela closed her eyes, silently praying for strength. It wouldn't need to take more than five seconds to cause mayhem. She'd already hovered on the precipice. The last few weeks had drained her. She constantly analyzed what they'd shared and what she could've done differently. She couldn't stop thinking that there'd been more. More emotion and affection. More connection sizzling under the surface.

Yes, she'd thought the same thing about Lucas, but once he'd passed, those feelings had, too. The reality of their marriage had bled into her memories, allowing her to see how wrong she'd been to expect anything more than friendship and sex from her husband. He'd been explicit. Not only in his words, but in his actions. He hadn't wanted anything from her. Not love. Not affection. Just someone to care for him in his final months. And not once had he wavered.

But with Bryan, she couldn't let go.

Everything between them was different. He contradicted the space he tried to place between them by selflessly pleasuring her, by listening to her past marriage problems, by taking the books that served as a painful reminder of Lucas and giving them away respectfully. He'd flirted with her, laughed, joked, bought wine and dinner. He'd taken her out. He'd desired her.

And those kisses. Every brush and sweep of his tongue had told a story about something more than sex.

"Whatever happened between you two, he's not coping, Pamela."

That made her eyes open and her heart climb to her throat. "What do you mean?"

"He had a scare today." Cassie straightened to her full height. "A panic attack. A complete meltdown. Or something similar. And he won't talk to any of us about it."

The heavy doses of affection for a man she'd tried to forget came rushing back in a torrential flood. "A panic attack?"

Cassie sighed. "It might not seem like a big deal, but for Bryan—"

"No. I get it." He was bound by control. Entirely guarded. If he'd broken, she knew it must be due to something unfathomably horrible. "What happened?" She didn't want to care, but she did. She cared so much her chest fractured a little.

"He left a work meeting early, which wasn't unexpected with his recent mood. He's been grumpier than usual since he canceled the demonstration night."

He'd canceled? Her insides grated over exposed heartstrings.

"You didn't know?" Cassie scrutinized her.

"No." Pamela shook her head. "But I'm nobody to him. There's no reason I should've known."

184

"I thought the two of you were close. Shay told me he had dinner at your apartment and took you to a bar. To him, that's—"

"Our time together was an effort to convince me to be his demo assistant. That's all. Nothing more."

"Right..." Cassie straightened. "I just thought—"

"Maybe something happened with his mother." She was sick of the speculation. Each question only made her stupidity more apparent. "He had a lot on his mind about his family."

"He told you about them?" Cassie frowned.

"Only about his mother's cancer. Maybe she took a turn, and he isn't taking it well." She shrugged, becoming increasingly overwhelmed with the layers of confusion and annoyance beaming back at her.

"He told you his mother has cancer?"

"Yeah... Why?" She shot a glance at Kim, wordlessly asking for emotional backup. "Doesn't she?"

"I don't know. Bryan has never spoken to me about his family. And from what T.J.'s mentioned, he hasn't brought up his parents in years."

"Oh..." Her mouth formed a circle that cemented in place.

"Yeah, *oh*. You seem to be the only person he's opened up to in a really long time."

"He didn't open up." The tiny glimpse of insight hadn't been anything remotely monumental. "It was a brief mention."

"A brief mention that his mom has cancer?" Cassie raised her brows. "Pamela, believe me, if he even mentioned his parents, he was opening up. He doesn't share information about his past. He barely shares anything at all."

The woman sighed and relaxed her worried expression. "Like I was saying, he left the meeting early and retreated to the office where he's been hibernating for weeks. Five minutes later, we hear a huge crash and rush upstairs to find him tearing the place apart. There were books and files everywhere. The desk had been cleared with everything shoved to the floor. Including this."

Cassie handed over the envelope again, and this time Pamela took it.

"Is he okay?"

"Physically, yes. But mentally? Emotionally? No." She shook her head. "I don't think he is. Not at all. But he won't talk to us. So, that's why I'm here. While the two of you were spending time together, he was happy."

"He told you that?"

Cassie released a huff of laughter. "No. Like I said, Bryan doesn't open up. We have to watch and take subtle hints. He started smiling instead of bearing his usual scowl. He was joking around a lot more, too. Leo and T.J. tracked his unusual behavior, and you were their conclusion." Cassie paused, probably waiting for a reaction Pamela wasn't willing to give. "You're the only one who's been close with him lately. Which is why I thought, if I came here and begged, maybe you'd speak to him."

Kim cleared her throat, the noise a subtle warning not to take the bait.

"Look, I understand your position and the concern." Pamela shot a look at her sister, then returned her focus to Cassie. "But what Bryan wants is for me to stay away. He made that clear."

"Are you sure? Telling you about his mother is a huge move for him. It's more than he's ever given me, and I've been his friend for years."

"Cassie, he literally slept with me and five seconds later told me our association was over. Five seconds," she repeated. "Maybe even two."

The woman winced.

"See?" She slid back to the coffee machine to keep her hands busy. "I'm sorry I can't help you."

"You won't even try?"

"Why is she obligated to?" Kim grated. "He discarded her like garbage."

"Don't—" Pamela pressed her lips tight, breathing through the need to defend him. Kim was right. But her stupid, idiotic heart didn't like hearing the truth from someone else.

"You like him." Cassie's expression softened, the friendship turning to compassion.

"Understatement." Kim scoffed.

"*Kim*." She scowled at her sister. "Go finish up out back."

"Sorry. Was that supposed to be a secret?"

No. But it was personal. She didn't want Cassie sliding her into the Brute-groupie category, even though that was exactly where she needed to be. "Give me a minute, okay?"

Her sister sighed and made for the kitchen doors.

"I'm sorry. I didn't mean to make this harder on you." Cassie's voice held sincerity. "If it makes you feel any better, I think you're the reason he's been in seclusion for the last few weeks. He's showing signs of heartbreak."

"Pfft. I'm not convinced he has a heart at all."

Cassie's lips thinned into a sad smile. "Do you really believe that?"

Yes.

No.

Christ, she didn't know what to believe anymore. "I think you need to ask him about his family. Maybe then he'll talk to you about his mother."

"Okay." Cassie gave a solemn nod. "But I still think he'd really appreciate seeing you."

"If he needs me, he knows where to find me."

"You've gotta understand, a man like Bryan won't ask for help in words. He's not going to blurt it out. What he's doing is showing how badly he needs someone, and the four of us—Shay, Leo, T.J., and myself—aren't good enough. He needs you."

"This isn't fair." If he'd made a mistake and wanted to see her again, he needed to come crawling back. Not the other way around.

"He's a good man, Pamela. He's one of the best. He just doesn't like to show it."

"I know." She'd figured that out herself, which had made his rejection all the harder to bear. He was a great guy, who shared a sexual attraction with her, and still he preferred to be alone.

Cassie backtracked toward the door. "Well, if you change your mind, or want to talk, you can always find me at the club."

"Wait." Pamela grabbed the envelope and rushed around the counter. "I don't want this."

"Then give it back to him. Or rip it up. Either way, I don't want it either." She continued onto the sidewalk. "It was nice seeing you." Cassie gave a gentle finger-wave, then walked out of view, leaving numbness in her wake.

There was no point running after her. There was no strength or energy.

"Goddamn it." Instead, she pulled the cafe doors shut and flicked over the closed sign.

"You're thinking about going to see him, aren't you?" Kim spoke from the kitchen.

"I can't help it." She rested her head against the glass. "If he's going through something..."

"What?" The swinging kitchen doors whooshed open. "What are you going to do for him?"

"I don't know." She turned and dragged her feet back to the coffee machine. "What if Cassie's right? What if he needs me?"

"Pamela." Her name was a placation.

"I know. I know." She pulled the basket toward her and peeked inside. "You think I'm doing the same thing I did with Lucas."

Kim approached, meeting her gaze from the other side of the counter. "Aren't you?"

"It's different."

"How?"

The one-word question required a far bigger answer. One she wasn't sure she could convey with conviction when everything was uncertain.

"Pamela? Explain it to me. Make me understand why you're doing this to yourself again."

"Because this time it was real," she admitted. "With Bryan, it wasn't just about hoping for more. I could actually feel it. I could've sworn he felt the same way."

She placed the envelope back in the basket.

"You were wrong before. You thought the same about Lucas."

"No. I expected the same from Lucas. But I never felt it, and he never once showed it. I stupidly thought he owed me his affection after everything I did for him. I became infatuated with the thought of us being in love. I know that now."

"And maybe in a few years' time, you'll have the hindsight to explain this situation, too."

Pamela cringed. She didn't want to think about Bryan for years. Not if she couldn't be with him.

"I want you to be happy." Kim gave a half-hearted smile. "After everything you've been through, you deserve someone who adores you."

"Then what should I do?"

"We should upgrade your standard pity party into something sponsored by your sexy club. Look." She pulled out one of the bottles from the basket. "We've got vodka."

"And wine."

"Two bottles." Kim waggled her brows. "And your light ass wouldn't even need one." She continued looking through the basket, her fingers pausing on the envelope. "Do you mind if I take a look? I've always wanted to know how much you pay to get laid."

Pamela rolled her eyes. "Go for it." She was curious to find out the monetary value herself. What price had he placed on her broken heart? Had he refunded her membership for the exact number of months she wouldn't attend? Or would he add more insult to her emotional injuries by giving her added compensation?

Kim carefully opened the back and pulled out a slip of paper, the piece no bigger than a business card. "Are you sure there's supposed to be a refund in here?"

"That's what Cassie said." She pressed onto the tips of her toes, trying to catch a glimpse of the contents.

"Well, this definitely isn't a check." Kim placed the paper back inside the envelope and handed it over. "Take a look."

It was a standard size, nothing special, apart from her full first name scribbled on the front. There was no nickname this time. And there was no check inside, either. Not even cash.

She retrieved the scrap of paper and felt the blood rush from her face. "A funeral notice..."

Her heart squeezed, tighter and tighter until she couldn't take it anymore. She blinked through her rapidly blurring vision to read the heartbreaking words resting in her palm.

MUNRO, *Pamela Sue of Tampa aged 55 years.*

Dearly loved wife of Raymond Thomas Munro. Mother of Bryan Munro. Cherished sister to Andrew and Kylie, and aunt to Silvia, Tyler, Jackson, and Tera.

Relatives and friends are respectfully invited to attend a funeral service for Pamela, which will be held in the chapel at 17 Day Street on the 1st of May, commencing at 10 a.m. to be followed by interment in the cemetery.

No flowers by request. Donations to your preferred cancer charity appreciated.

"His mom," she whispered. That's why he'd always called her Ella. "She must've died weeks ago. Around the same time I ignored his text message." Guilt and regret bubbled inside her, coming out in the form of a dry sob.

He'd reached out. He'd wanted a shoulder. And she'd ignored him.

"Hey, now. Don't get crazy." Kim came around the counter. "I'm sure he's fine."

"But he's not. Didn't you hear what Cassie said? He's falling apart and won't even talk to his friends about it. They don't even know his mother died."

"And what makes you think he'll talk to you? You're only going to get hurt."

Too late. She was already straddling heartache and limbo. "I need to see him."

"Sweetie..." Kim placed a gentle hand on her elbow. "Please don't."

"You know I have to do this. I can't keep questioning myself. Either way, I have to get answers." She grabbed her handbag from under the register. "Would you mind closing up for me?"

"Only if you call as soon as you finish talking to him." Kim placed her hands on her hips. "And grant me permission to knee-cap him if he upsets you."

"He's grieving—"

"Kneecaps or no deal."

"Fine. You can do whatever you like if this turns sour." She'd deal with the possibility of having to lie to her sister later. For now, she had to get to the club. To ease her pain, and hopefully his. "I'll call you as soon as I'm done."

CHAPTER SEVENTEEN

*B*ryan stared at the mess once known as the work office. He'd lost his mind. Momentarily. Now the remnants of their once tidy work space lay scattered across the floor in a mangled heap that mimicked his life.

All because of a death notice.

A death notice he couldn't fucking find.

"It has to be here somewhere." The new envelope was missing. The one he'd written on. Those six letters to name the person who left his life long ago, but shaped every decision he'd ever made. She was the reason he'd never had a relationship. She'd created his paranoia over love and commitment, and molded him into the man who refused to let down his guard.

All for what? Stubborn pride? Superiority? To continue a fight with his parents, when the assholes didn't even know they were still at war?

They never gave a shit about the years he'd spent distancing himself from others in retaliation to what they'd put him through. They didn't care enough to pay attention.

The ongoing barrage of reminders made him want to tear

apart the office all over again. He wanted to destroy everything. Most of all, his mother. But evidently, she was already dead, and probably looking up from hell with just as much disdain for him as she always had.

"It's not in here, man. Maybe Shay or Cassie thought it was rubbish." Leo kicked at a splayed book on the floor. "What was in the envelope, anyway?"

He huffed out a breath. "Nothing." He wouldn't check the bin for a third time when the first two attempts came up empty.

"You lost your shit looking for an envelope with nothing in it?" T.J. shot a glance at Leo, the two of them sharing a silent communication.

"Yeah, I guess I did." He strode for the door, still incapable of revealing the bullshit clogging his veins. He couldn't talk about it. He didn't even understand it. "I've gotta get out of here. I'll clean this mess up later."

They didn't stop him. Didn't say a word. Their kid gloves were well and truly in place, with neither of them willing to give him the verbal beatdown he deserved for destroying their space. Shay and Cassie hadn't chastised him when they'd walked in on his meltdown, either.

He fled down the hall, then took the stairs to Shot of Sin two at a time. He should've run. Instead, he decided to hide. He practically jogged across the empty dance floor, unlocked the Vault door, and descended the next staircase in darkness.

He didn't bother with the lights. He hoped he'd fall. A few broken bones and a heavy sedative seemed preferable to the punishing void consuming him.

His mother was dead, and the web-thin ties connecting him to the rest of his family had been severed. The news should've brought delirious joy. Somehow, it didn't. Now, there was another layer to his lack of worth. Another brick to add to the wall around him.

He reached the bottom of the stairs intact and slammed his way through the next pin-code door until he reached the newbie lounge. After a slap against the light switch, he continued into the main room, then straight behind the bar.

Instinct had him reaching for a bottle of scotch, dragging the soothing liquid to stand on the counter in front of him. He stared at the alcohol, his body begging for a taste, his mind pleading for the escapism.

He wouldn't be defeated.

This time, he'd savor the new invisible scars his parents had inflicted on him with pure lucidity. He'd relish the pain. He'd make the torment solidify his strength and wash away the momentary lapse when he'd stupidly decided to give a fuck about someone.

He became infatuated with the bottle, entranced by the possible solace for minutes. Maybe hours. Then the main entrance door squeaked and he closed his eyes, not wanting to face whoever came to break his solitude.

"I thought I'd find you down here."

Cassie.

Out of all the people to disturb him, it had to be her.

They should've sent Shay. He'd have no hesitation in giving Leo's girlfriend a piece of his mind. But Cassie was different. She was soft. Kind. A fucking burst of unwanted sunshine.

He opened his eyes and visually defiled the scotch. "This is the only time I'm allowed down here, remember?"

"I was under the impression the hiatus was your choice."

"My choice?" Maybe it was. If only he hadn't pissed off the women of the Vault in the first place. If only he'd sent one of the security team after Ella that night in the parking lot instead of indulging his unprecedented interest in someone of the opposite sex.

"I thought you were hiding from something," Cassie hedged. "Or someone."

He squeezed the neck of the bottle, not appreciating her accuracy.

It wasn't that he was hiding from Ella. He knew he wouldn't see her again. Instead, he supposed he was withdrawing from anyone or anything that reminded him of his mistakes.

"I just want to be left alone."

Slowly, she came toward the bar, her eyes bleeding with concern as she took a seat on the stool opposite him. "I went to see Pamela today."

Every muscle snapped rigid. The anger and self-loathing fled under the weight of panic. Pure fear. "Why?"

"I thought I'd make things easier on you and drop off her refund."

"Thanks," the word grated through his teeth. "But I could've done it. It was only a case of writing a check and putting it in the mail. I wasn't going to see her."

Cassie shrugged. "I figured as much. That's why I knew it was the right decision. We were all concerned that things didn't end amicably."

He narrowed his eyes, giving a voiceless warning.

"Not between you and her," she quickly amended. "Between the Vault itself. You know how much we pride ourselves on the club's reputation."

His jaw ached under the pressure of his clenched molars. "I hope you were smart enough to mind your own business, Cass."

She broke eye contact, her chin hitching in the slightest show of remorseful defiance.

"*Cassie?*" His blood surged.

Her cheeks turned a warm shade of pink, and the delicate

column of her throat rolled with a heavy swallow. "You haven't been yourself lately. I thought she was the cause."

"But now you know better." It should've been a statement. He should've spoken with conviction. Instead, he was stuck sounding like a jackass as he waited for her to spill whatever news she had about the woman who hijacked his masculinity.

"Now I know something special happened between the two of you. You like her, Bryan. I know you do. And when I handed over the check you wrote, I could tell she was upset by the formality."

There were many things to hate about her statement, but his focus pinpointed the abnormality. "I didn't write a check, Cassie. I hadn't gotten around to it."

Her eyes met his, her brows knitting tight.

Something was wrong with this situation. Something his intuition had already begun to digest with nauseous anticipation.

"I found the envelope you addressed to her. It was on the floor in the office."

On the floor.

In his office.

There were no words. Only panic. Only volatile anger.

"Bryan?"

His lungs heaved with each breath. His limbs shook. He gripped the counter behind him with his free hand, that liquor bottle burning a hole through his other palm. "It wasn't a fucking check."

The bottle threatened to slide from his grip. He tightened his hold, clutching the glass to stop himself from throwing it against the wall.

Ella had his mother's death notice.

"Did you see her open it?"

She shook her head.

Maybe there was still time to get the envelope before it was opened. To reclaim his privacy.

"Go get it." He glared to reiterate the demand.

"I'm sorry, Bryan. I thought I was doing the right thing."

"No, you didn't. You didn't give a shit about the right thing. You only wanted to sate your curiosity."

She cringed. "You've never made friends with a woman before. Not like this. At least, not that I've ever known. And you were happy. Then, all of a sudden, you cancel the demo night and start falling into a spiraling depression. I wanted to know what happened. We all needed to make sure you were okay."

He stepped toward her side of the bar, raising to his full height. "Get it back. *Now*."

"I..." She cleared her throat. "It was almost closing time. She wouldn't be there anymore."

"Then find her. Get in your car and don't come back until you have it."

Her eyes glistened, the slight sheen of approaching tears kicking him square in the balls. *Fucking hell.* He swung away, facing the back of the bar, the bottle now a serious temptation in his closed fist.

If he started drinking, he wouldn't stop. Not today. Not tomorrow.

"What was in the envelope? What's so important?" Her voice shook. "And why didn't she know the demonstration night was canceled? What happened between you two? One minute you were dating. The next you were—"

"We weren't dating." He hung his head.

"I disagree." Her voice continued to waver, but there was backbone in her words. "You told her things. You cared for her. I didn't need to see the two of you together to come to that conclusion. I've heard parts of what happened. You went to her cafe, and her house. You brought food and wine. Then a few days later, you're taking her to a bar. How isn't that dating?"

He didn't know. He'd never dated before.

"You chased her, Bryan. You went after her because you like her. You may have blamed it on a million different reasons, but you enjoyed her company and you wanted to keep—"

"Enough."

"No. You need to realize—"

"*I fucking realize, okay?*" His head pounded through the admission, each heartbeat bringing the threat of a stroke. "I know."

"So, you realize you like her?"

Christ, did she want him to carve the declaration into his flesh? "I *realize*."

"And you're going to let her get away?"

"She's already gone." He shrugged. "There's nothing I can do."

"You pushed her away. But I don't think it was hard enough to be permanent. You could get her back."

Why? For what reason other than to drag her down to his heartless level? "I don't want her back." He only wanted to know what she'd said. How she'd said it. And what she'd looked like when those words had left her lips.

"Why?"

He scoffed. There were a hundred and one reasons. A thousand. Many more. "Because it's a waste of time. Everyone walks away in the end."

"How can you say that? Especially after everything T.J. and I went through. We went to hell and back, and now look at us."

He should've clarified—everyone walked away from *him*. His parents. His aunts and uncles. His cousins.

He turned to face her, taking in the determined set of her shoulders. "Cass, T.J. tried like hell to leave you behind."

"You know that's a lie." Her eyes sparked with defensive rage. "He was only doing it to protect me."

The inside door squeaked again, making his exhaustion peak. If Shay added to this bullshit, he'd lose his fucking mind. More than he already had.

"You need to get my envelope back." He jerked his chin toward the internal door to the upstairs staircase. "And take whoever that is with you. I'm not interested in company."

A curvy figure came to stand in the doorway to the newbie lounge, the familiarity setting his vision to flame.

Fuck. Me.

He stumbled back to the counter and gripped the scotch like a lifeline. His throat threatened to close. His lungs demanded more air.

Cassie swiveled on the stool, the name she spoke slicing through him like a sword through silk. "Pamela."

"Hey." The response was the sweetest form of torture. A punishment he couldn't keep his gaze from.

"What are you doing here?" The question was born from habit. He already knew the answer. He just needed to fill the void of restricting silence. "I thought you weren't coming back."

"I heard you had a bad day." She held up the envelope in her hand. "I read about it, too. But don't worry, I overheard you say you didn't want company. I promise I won't stay long." She was fragile—her eyes, her lips. Even her skin seemed like porcelain. Her attention gently raked over him, tearing through skin, ripping through flesh. "Can we talk?"

He couldn't deny her. He couldn't watch her walk away again. Not yet, anyway. "Give us a minute, Cass."

"Okay." She gave a hollow nod and slid from the stool.

"Please make sure you don't run out of here without saying goodbye."

He couldn't make any promises. Not that it would matter. By the time he was ready to flee, Cassie would have Shay, T.J., and Leo positioned at the exits, ensuring he couldn't escape unnoticed. "We'll catch up later."

"Thank you." She strode for Ella, giving the other woman's shoulder a squeeze as she passed before disappearing into the newbie lounge.

The room closed in around him, those eyes reading him and finding the truth.

He couldn't do this. Not today.

He cracked the cap of the scotch and took a long pull. The burn lessened the emotional carnage staring him in the face, but one taste wasn't enough. He feared the whole bottle wouldn't dint the surface of the shit-storm about to descend.

"Did you tell them?" Slowly, she approached the bar, her work pants stained with coffee, her white button-down wrinkled at the ends. He loved that she wasn't picture-perfect. Mascara smudged her eyelids. If she'd worn lipstick today, it was nowhere to be seen. Not that she needed it. Her lips had always been her most endearing feature. Hypnotic and too damn influential.

"What's there to tell?"

"You've kept the information to yourself this whole time?" She rounded the bar, stopping a few feet away.

"This whole time?" He gave a harsh laugh and downed another gulp of awaiting solace. "I guess I enjoy my privacy too much."

"Then I assume you didn't want me to have this." She placed the envelope on the counter, her hand lingering against the name written on the front.

"Cassie had no business going to see you."

She winced, the slightest furrow marring her brow. Her

pain was more torturous than the threat of Cassie's tears. Ella's discomfort tore at him, demanding apology, which he beat back with another quick pull from the bottle.

"You should slow down with the alcohol." She eyed the sloshing liquid. "You're going to feel crappy tomorrow. There's no point making it worse."

"There are only two things I need at the moment, and one of them is booze." Lucidity was no longer an option with her here. She was still fuckable. Still irresistible.

"And the other?"

"Sex."

It was a taunt. He couldn't help it. Making the conversation interesting saved his mind from the dark and dreary cave of reality. And, truth be told, even though they were discussing his mother, he wasn't even thinking of her. There was only Ella.

"Well, you've got a bar full of booze." She glanced around the room, probably searching for a diversion. "And you've already made it clear I can't help with the other matter. So, I guess you want me to leave."

He couldn't tell if she was itching for a fight or an excuse to run. He could never tell with her. "I'm not going to kick you out. Feel free to pull up a stool and take a front row seat to my impending alcoholism." He swung the bottle to his lips, watching her as he took another long pull. "You'll probably enjoy the show after all the shit I've put you through."

"What shit?"

He released a breath of a laugh. "I don't need to paint you a picture. We were both there."

"Oh, no." She shook her head and crossed her arms over her chest. "That's not what I meant. I'm just trying to figure out which shitty moment you're referring to."

This time his laugh was audible. "I appreciate the honesty."

"I'm not going to coddle you." She approached, her steps still slow and cautious. "But I do think you need to add some water to your intake." She reached out, her warm fingers brushing his to grip the bottle neck. "Let me take this."

She kept their hands fused, their eyes, too. "Please." She tilted the scotch, inching it toward her chest. One hard tug had it slipping through his fingers, and she placed the bottle gently on the bar beside them.

He could give up the liquor if he didn't lose the heat of her. Denying himself both didn't seem fair.

"Bryan..."

The whisper of his name brought pain. Nobody had ever spoken to him like that. Not without desire or need. She was selflessly here, dealing with his shit, and he couldn't understand why.

"Why do you care?" He inched closer, his thigh brushing hers, the zing of atomic attraction washing away the fucked-up reasons that drove him to drink in the first place.

She didn't retreat, only hitched her chin higher, refusing to look away. "You need water."

"It doesn't even rank in the top twenty things I need."

"Really?" This time she stepped back, and he countered with an arm around her waist, keeping them close.

"Yeah. Really."

She elbowed him, soft but blunt. "You're looking for a distraction, which will only be temporary. You need to talk this out. If not to me, then your friends. Tell them about the cancer. Tell them about the funeral."

"I didn't go."

She balked, her lashes rapidly beating in a show of shock.

The seconds of silence were punishing. For once, he didn't want her thinking he was a callous asshole. He didn't enjoy the judgment staring back at him. He wanted to be better. To be worthy. "I didn't know about it. They didn't tell me."

"They didn't tell you when they were holding the funeral of your own mother?"

No. For the first time, someone in his family had heard his voice, even though his request had been a painful backlash. They always found his weak spot, no matter how he acted.

"They didn't tell me she was dead."

Her expression fell, her throat churning over a heavy swallow. Breath by agonizing breath, her devastation reigniting his own. "When did you find out?"

"A few hours before you did."

Her gorgeous face bleached, all color and compassion. She turned away, gripped the counter, and released a long breath before sucking in another lungful of air.

"Ella?" He placed the bottle beside her and ran his palm over her arm. "What's going on? Why are you upset?"

"Why?" She slid farther along the bar. "I'm devastated for you. You don't deserve this. They put you through enough already. I don't understand..."

He became lost in her words and the tears now staining her cheeks. She was crying. Not because of something he'd done. Those tears seemed to be due to something she felt.

For him.

She cared?

About him?

"There's no point crying a river, sweetheart. It's not like I want to bring her back. My mother is exactly where she deserves to be."

"Oh, God." Her eyes widened. "Don't say that."

"Why? I didn't kill her. I'm just not sorry she's gone."

"You're grieving, Bryan."

"Not for her." He shook his head. He felt something, but it definitely wasn't grief for the woman who'd birthed him. "I swear I couldn't give a shit about her passing."

"Then what happened earlier today?"

Earlier today? He ran over the day's events, pinpointing the only thing worthy of making the rumor mill. "Fucking Cassie. What did she say?"

"She was worried about you."

"Well, for the sake of my sanity, can we please ignore every other motherfucker on the face of the planet for the time being?"

"*I'm* worried about you."

Jesus Christ. Where the hell did he put the scotch?

"I don't know what else to tell you." He ran a hand through his hair, unable to explain his confusion. He'd never given a shit about his mother. He didn't care about her death. It was something else. Something he couldn't pinpoint.

"When Lucas died, I cried for days, even though we were never close." Her voice came in slow, soft bursts. The depressing lilt reeked of despair. "It wasn't until a week later that I realized I was grieving more for what could've been. I was hurting because the dreamy relationship I fought for us to have would never happen. I'd tried so hard to get him to love me, never giving up hope it would happen one day. Then he was gone. And so were all the fairytale dreams." She lowered her gaze, staring at her feet. "I grieved for what could've been. Not the man who died... If that makes sense."

He froze, her explanation sinking down to his marrow.

It was such simple insight. So easily spoken. Yet, it was exactly how he felt. He didn't give a fuck about his egg donor. The thing tearing him apart was what he'd missed. What most people took for granted.

A pained laugh escaped, the action dislodging the ache behind his ribs. He couldn't fathom the brilliance of this woman. He didn't know why she knew his thoughts, or how she'd become abnormally insightful. He just loved the fact she was here, with him, pushing away the hollow feeling that no longer dictated his chest.

"Did I overstep?" She glanced up at him through thick lashes, the sight of her concern depriving him of words. "I'm sorry... I should go."

He couldn't make her stay.

He *shouldn't*.

"Again," she added softly, "I'm sorry for what you're going through. It gets easier. I promise." She made for the end of the counter, her retreat encouraging the return of his hollow torment.

He needed her here. And yet, he didn't have any way to encourage her to stick around.

There were no bonus points for enduring his company. He didn't have the kindhearted nature of T.J. or the smooth sophistication of Leo.

Only a shitty attitude and an even shittier outlook on life.

"Don't." That was all he had. One word. One pathetic, timid syllable.

She paused, her back to him, her hands limp at her sides. He could feel her slipping away, moving closer and closer toward an escape even though she remained in place.

"Stay a while." He came up behind her and wove a hand around her hip.

The only asset in his arsenal was sex.

Carnal finesse.

The gift of orgasms.

She gave an audible swallow, and he fought the need to cringe. Everything about her spoke of discomfort—her stiff spine, her rushed breathing, her silence.

She turned, her hip brushing his crotch with painful effect. The slight connection had his cock filling with rapidly-pulsing blood. Those dark lashes beating up at him made coherence difficult.

"You want a distraction?"

"I want you." He pulled her tight against him and clasped the back of her neck with his free hand.

"What about your insurance policy?"

He scoffed. "Turns out all bets are off when you find out your mother is six feet under."

She cringed. Maybe she didn't appreciate his callousness, or sensed his lie. But the evidence stood thick and heavy between them, his dick taking center stage as he leaned in to slant his mouth over hers.

The kiss was utter finesse—smooth swipes of lips and a gentle dance of tongues. He wanted to tattoo this moment on her soul. To engrave himself in her memory, like she'd carved a hole in his.

"Stop." She placed her hands on his chest. "I still don't think this is a good idea."

The rejection stung deeper than it should have. "Why? It's not like my track record has provided anything but satisfaction."

She scowled. Scoffed. The two reactions kneeing him in the conscience.

"*Fuck*." He stepped back. "I'm sorry. I'm shitty company today... As opposed to every other day, right?"

He waited for her to retaliate. For those eyes to continue spitting fire.

"I never minded your company, Bryan."

"Skip the placations, sweetheart. We both know I pissed you off more often than not. It's what I do."

Her shoulders slumped, his words defeating her in a way he didn't understand. "You're nicer than you think you are."

"Then sleep with me," he begged. The sorry sack of shit he'd turned into pleaded to get laid. Not by anyone. Only her. Only because he presumed he'd never get the opportunity again. "Neither one of us has anything to lose."

Her smile was fake. Maybe even reminiscent. "Bryan, if I tell you what's going on in my mind, it will reinstate your insurance policy."

"Then don't." He slid toward her, smashing his lips to hers, lifting her off the ground. "Don't say a word."

"I can't keep this to myself." Those determined hands found his chest again, pushing. "If we don't see each other again, I want to make sure this is out in the open."

She was seeing someone. Fucking someone.

Christ, he didn't want to know who.

"Bryan?"

"Yeah?" He placed her on her feet and reached for the bottle of scotch, letting the burning liquid unleash on his throat.

"You're not going to want to hear this."

He nodded, his focus on the dwindling scotch.

She was right. He was already prepared to tell her to leave without explanation. He didn't want to hear the details of who she'd hooked up with. Could it be the cowboy from the bar? Or the weak bastard who fumbled over his words out the front of her cafe? Maybe it was someone with worse qualities.

God knew she had shitty taste in men.

"All right. Let me have it." He raised the bottle again, this time holding the liquid in his mouth, letting it sauté his tongue.

"I like you."

The alcohol gagged him, choking the air from his lungs. "What?"

"When we first met, I promised I had no interest in you —not because I knew that was what you wanted to hear—I actually didn't like you. I thought your attitude was toxic and your confidence grated on my nerves. But the man I got to know is nothing like the brute everyone claims you are." She nibbled her lower lip. "I don't see that guy when I look at you. I see someone I want to spend more time with. Someone I fell for. Someone I could see myself falling in love with."

He dropped the bottle to the counter, still clutching the neck for grounding.

"Don't get angry." She held her hands up in surrender. "I know it's the last thing you want to hear. And that's why I didn't tell you the night in the parking lot. I walked away, just like you wanted me to. But I can't be with you tonight and pretend I feel differently. I can't lie by omission."

He wanted to believe everything he heard. If it wasn't for the alcohol, the nervous breakdown, and the fucked-up news about his mother, he probably could've convinced himself this wasn't a hallucination. Problem was, it seemed too coincidental to have the one thing he wanted laid out before him within accessible reach. It was too good to be true.

"Say something," she pleaded.

"Give me a second." His head spun, liquor and disorientation having their wicked way with him.

He wanted to sober up. He *needed* to sober up.

He side-stepped to the sink, snatched an empty glass from the rack, and filled it with water. Gulp after gulp, he downed one glass, then two, his impatience making the numbing intoxication a heavy liability.

"Don't worry about it." Her voice drifted. "I'll see myself out."

"*No.*" God, no. He just needed a minute.

He gripped the counter, lowered his head and breathed deep.

"It's okay. This response is better than the rage I anticipated. I thought you'd yell at me."

Because that was what he'd done in the past. It was all he knew how to do.

Focus.

He mentally repeated a suitable response, over and over, to make sure it seemed worthy. "I feel the same way."

She was quiet, deathly silent.

He glanced from the corner of his eye to find confusion staring back at him. He didn't know if he'd spoken aloud or if the mantra in his head had grown in strength.

She didn't acknowledge him. She probably didn't know what he was talking about because all the things she'd said were a figment of his imagination.

Fuck.

"Ella?" He straightened and told his insecurities to fuck off. "I feel the same way."

CHAPTER EIGHTEEN

*P*amela held herself in check.

Bryan was drunk and on emotional life-support, making her blurted confession a disaster waiting to happen.

"It's your turn to say something," he whispered.

Her lips quirked, the burn of tears returning to her eyes. "I'm still trying to digest what you said."

"Why?"

"You're confused—"

"About the way I feel?" He spoke with vehemence. "No shit. I've spent the weeks trying to figure it out, and it still doesn't make sense."

All her needy insecurities latched on with energetic force. "You've been thinking about me for weeks?"

"You sound pleased to know I haven't had a lick of sleep since I last saw you." He bridged the gap between them, the tips of his shoes nudging hers. "And people think I'm the brutal one."

This time her smile flourished, spreading across her face in unmanageable enthusiasm. "You're not brutal."

"Don't go ruining my reputation, sweetheart." He backed her into the counter, his hips rocking into hers. "You've done enough to me already."

His strength seeped into her, calming the frazzled nerves and heartache. She wanted to fall deeper into him, to sink, to drown. But she couldn't. Not yet.

"Can we put this on hold for a while?"

He slid his hands into hers, entwining their fingers against her thighs. "You still think this is a reaction to grief?"

She nodded. "A little."

"That's okay." He grinned, surprising her with the impressive display. "I still think it's a drunken hallucination."

He pressed his lips to hers, stealing away the negative thoughts with his patented kissing style. He licked her thoroughly, patiently, their tongues sparring and dancing. She ran her hands along the lapels of his suit, holding him close, but a distant sound disturbed her concentration, the murmurs of conversation building with every second.

Bryan broke the kiss to glare over her shoulder. "Your cavalry has arrived."

She frowned and turned to find Leo, T.J., Cassie, and Shay striding into the main room, only to freeze in place, one after the other.

"Whoa." T.J. shot a glance at his wife. "This isn't what I expected to find."

"What *did* you expect?" Bryan caged Pamela in place from behind, one hand on the counter at either side of her hips.

"I, umm..." Cassie blushed. "I thought it was a good idea to do a welfare check. Things were tense earlier."

"We're okay." Pamela straightened, keeping the heat of Bryan tight at her back. "Everything is fine."

Cassie nodded while Shay crossed her arms over her chest.

"Cue the questions," Bryan muttered in her ear.

"Is your mom okay?" Shay asked. "Apparently, you told Pamela she was sick."

"*Shay*," Cassie hissed. "That was private."

Shit. Bryan remained quiet, his warmth turning to icy steel.

"I'm sorry." She turned in his arms. "I mentioned it to Cassie earlier. I assumed they already knew." She held her breath, waiting for his anger.

"Don't worry." He gave her a thin-lipped smile. "Shay snoops like a P.I. She would've found out sooner or later."

His easy acceptance only compiled her guilt. It also made her want to kiss the breath from his lungs.

"Is she okay?" Leo asked.

Bryan kept his focus on her, not acknowledging his friends as he announced, "She's dead."

She didn't wince. Didn't flinch. She began to think the brutal replies were the only way he knew how to respond. Maybe it was a coping mechanism, or something he'd been taught since childhood from his heartless parents.

"Oh, shit." T.J.'s voice sounded over the numerous gasps. "What happened?"

Bryan's composure fractured, his forehead creasing with deep wrinkles.

"It's okay." She could be his strength. At least, she wanted to be if he'd allow her. "Let me take care of it." She faced his friends with a sad smile. "She lost her battle with cancer at the end of April."

"April?" Shay accused. "She died last month and you couldn't tell us?"

Pamela flinched, her blood boiling over the insensitive reaction.

"Let her go," Bryan mumbled in her ear, his arm weaving around her waist. "I get too much satisfaction watching her make an ass of herself."

"Brute?" Shay snapped. "What the hell?"

"You've gotta admit, this is unfair," Leo added. "We've given you space for weeks, letting you dump the workload on our shoulders. I don't doubt you needed time, but you could've told us before today. We had no idea what was going on."

Bryan began playing with her hair, acting as though the heated conversation was a casual chit-chat. "This pretty little lady was the cause of my issues. Not my mother."

"Me?" She peered over her shoulder. "Why?"

"I told you—you were messing with my head. I couldn't concentrate. I had to bow out of dealing with customers because my public relation skills became less than stellar."

"They've never been anything to write home about," Shay muttered.

He smirked, the expression quickly fading. "I didn't find out about my mother until today."

"Oh, shit." Leo palmed his stubbled jaw. "Who the fuck does that?"

"My family," Bryan offered. "But on the bright side—one down, one to go."

They all cringed.

Leo held up his hands in warning. "Don't say shit like that. You're gonna go to hell."

"At least my family will be there to greet me, right?"

"Bryan..." Her plea whispered between them. She couldn't handle his detachment anymore. It wasn't healthy. She needed them to be alone so she could comfort him the way women do—with affection and understanding and love. Not the careless back and forth between friends.

Cassie met her gaze, her eyes questioning. "We should go back upstairs..."

"*Yes. Please,*" she mouthed, appreciating the woman's intuition. "*Thank you.*"

"Good idea. We'll give you two a few more minutes alone." T.J. placed a hand on his wife's hip and guided her toward the exit. "If you need anything..."

"I'm good." Bryan's lie was convincing. If only she didn't know better.

"Yeah." Leo nodded. "We're here, buddy. Just say the word."

The four of them filed through the entry to the newbie lounge, their footsteps fading until the deafening click of a door latch sealed her fate.

The room remained silent, the emptiness closing in on her as Bryan's heartbeat echoed into her back. She sensed he wouldn't fill the void. At least not with honesty or emotion. If she left the conversation up to him, she was certain there'd be more dark humor to mask his feelings. She craved his trust and wished he would open up to her. Even if just a little.

"You joke about things that upset you."

He nestled his forehead into her hair. "It's what I do."

"If you talk it out, it might get better." She stared across the room, knowing he'd loathe her suggestion.

"I prefer my way. It works for me." A way that kept his heartbreak hidden and slowly building. God forbid he ruined his reputation. "For now," he added. "Who knows what girly things you'll talk me into if we start spending more time together."

"Is that what you want?" She turned, becoming ensnared in the emotional depth of his eyes. There was no more dark or callous banter. He was bare, vulnerable, and oh, so beautiful. "The time together, not the girly part."

"That's what comes next, right? I've never done this before."

"That's not what I asked. I want to know what *you* want."

One side of his lips gradually kicked, his smirk building as he pressed his hips harder into hers. "In that case, I think we both know the answer."

"*Bryan.*" She struggled not to laugh. "I'm serious."

He stared at her mouth, his thumb lifting to trace her lower lip with feather-light pressure. "You still want to wait?"

"That depends..."

His gaze snapped to hers. "On?"

"On whether you want me to feel secure in what's going on between us. The physical part has been easy. Why don't we give ourselves time to work on everything else?"

"You're trying to appeal to logic over my libido?" He clucked his tongue. "Stupid move, sweetheart."

It wasn't stupid. She wanted him to be of sound mind the next time they slept together. For her sake, and his. Regret was the last thing either one of them needed if he woke up tomorrow and decided he'd made a mistake. "I just thought waiting would be best."

He ignored her and leaned in to trek his lips along her jaw, to her neck, then the sensitive spot below her ear.

Alcohol. Bereavement. Heartache. She reminded herself of the aspects shaping his decisions.

She shouldn't encourage his heavenly seduction. Not when he was finally where he was supposed to be. She should hold out, for her heart's sake. For one more day. At least until morning.

"Tomorrow, you'll have more clarity. More stability." She sighed as his mouth found her collarbone, the rough scrape of beard adding a touch of friction to the exquisite softness of his kisses.

"Right."

His thigh parted hers, the rub against the crotch of her pants grazing her clit. Tingles spread through her abdomen, the tendrils of pleasure creeping higher and higher. Slowly, her brain switched gears, sliding commonsense to the sideline and yanking gratification to the forefront. She needed more touches, more kisses, more endorphins.

He pulsed his leg between hers, taunting her pussy. "More security?"

"Mmm hmm." She closed her eyes and whimpered. Hope was lost. Not one single part of her body wanted to be apart from this man. Not one finger. Not one nerve.

Rational thought became suffocated by lust.

They could work out the important stuff tomorrow.

After.

"I guess I've been wrong before." Christ, she was such an easy mark. Such a groupie.

He didn't acknowledge her surrender, only continued the delicious trail of his mouth. She undid the top button of her shirt, then the next, exposing her cleavage to his mercy.

"I've dreamed about these." He slid his hand into the cup of her bra and brushed her nipple between his fingers. "My imagination didn't do them justice."

He kissed her sternum, the curve of her breast, then yanked at her bra to suck her nipple into his mouth. Wildfire flickered to life under her ribs. Passion collided with happiness.

For one tiny moment, everything was perfect. They were synced—movements, heartbeats, intensity. Mind, body, soul.

He paid homage to her breasts. His thigh teased her pussy. Every nerve tingled under his mastery. She could almost come like this, from friction and suction.

"We better get going." He straightened and stepped back, his lust seeming to vanish in an instant while she spun from the stronghold. "Let's get out of here."

"Excuse me?" She licked her drying lips as he grabbed the bottle of scotch and placed it in a cupboard under the bar. "What just happened?"

"You don't want to have sex. So, let's go."

"But..." How did he jump from the sizzling depths of carnality, to the freezing icecaps of chastity? "What? Why?"

"Your rules."

"Wow." Her mouth gaped. "You're horrible."

A picture-perfect grin beamed back at her. "Just in control for now."

"For now?"

"Yep. It doesn't always happen around you." He fastened her shirt buttons, the composed action a physical brag about his discipline. "Did you really think I'd risk all that stability and clarity you were mumbling about?"

"Then why start?"

"I'm not a priest." He winked. "You might dictate the rules, but I know how to play the game." He grabbed her hand and dragged her forward.

"That's a really nasty thing to do." Her panties were damp. Her breasts screamed for more. "I don't want to forgive you."

"I'm drunk and emotional, remember? Go easy on me."

"You're drunk, emotional, and soon to be neutered if you don't quit dragging me around."

"Neutering me would mean coming in close contact with my dick, and that's off limits. You can't break your own rules." He kept tugging, leading her around the bar toward the cement staircase leading to the Shot of Sin parking lot. "And besides, you like holding my hand."

"I can't believe you played me." She glared through an unwanted smile. "This isn't fair."

But it was. For once, everything seemed fair, and honest, and fun. Breathing him in, feeling his strength, knowing he cared—the happiness of it was overwhelming.

He paused at the foot of the staircase, the atmosphere changing as he focused into the darkness ahead. "Ella?"

His ominous tone killed her playful heartbeat. "Yeah?"

He shot her a glance over his shoulder, his features tight. "I can't promise I won't fuck this up."

Her heart swelled, the rush of blood struggling to get through. "I know."

He gave a sharp nod and continued forward, his fingers gently squeezing hers.

"Bryan?"

"Mmm?" He kept walking, bringing them to the top of the staircase and the door leading outside.

She wrapped her arms around his waist and nuzzled her head into his neck. "I can't promise I'll walk away the next time you ask me to."

"I can handle that."

"No." She shook her head. "I mean it. I'll put all those other sex hounds to shame."

He laughed and pushed opened the door. "Come on. Let's get out of here."

"I'm serious." She followed him into the dwindling daylight. "If you ever break up with me, I'll stalk you."

His snicker was awkward.

"And if you leave me, I'll slash your tires." She swung their joined hands with delight. "After all this time, destiny has finally brought us together." She grinned as he slowed his stride, his posture stiffening. "Do you think it's time to start discussing matching tattoos?"

He stopped, his gaze taking long seconds to meet hers. He scanned her face, searching her expression.

"What's wrong?" She blinked up at him. "Are you scared of needles?"

His eyes narrowed, and he yanked her into his chest. "You're playing games with me?"

"Maybe." She chuckled. "You started it."

"I'll finish it, too." He pinned her hands behind her back and smashed his mouth to hers, punishing her with bliss.

She wiggled, not wanting to succumb a second time. "Don't start this again."

"I won't." He stared down at her, his gaze raking over her eyes, her nose, her lips. Each feature was treated to the same visual affection. "I think I changed my mind."

"About?" She gave his gorgeous face the same tender inspection, taking in the kindness of those deep blue eyes and the dark tempting lips.

"I'm not going to fuck this up, Ella."

"You know what, Bryan?" Her heart swelled again, pumping tingling blood through every inch of her, filling her with confidence. "I believe you."

EPILOGUE

*P*amela slid her bare thighs onto the bar stool, feigning relaxation even though the sensation was illusive. Whimpers and groans filled her ears, along with murmured chatter, soft laughter, and the occasional clink of a glass as Vault patrons socialized around her.

"I didn't expect to see you down here." Shay retrieved a tall glass from the clean rack. "Tequila sunrise?"

"Yes, please." On second thought... "Make that a double."

Shay eyed her with suspicion. "Nervous to be back?"

"I'm not sure." She hadn't stepped foot inside the sex club in months. Not since the night she'd vowed never to return.

Life was different now. *Everything* was different. And knowing what to expect once she walked down the dimly lit Vault staircase had become an elaborate guessing game.

"Bryan told me the two of you stopped dating." Shay continued her scrutiny as she pulled a bottle of orange juice from the fridge under the counter.

"He did?"

"I didn't get the details. He only said the first date failed

221

with fucking brilliant efficiency, and he wouldn't be doing it again."

Pamela winced at the memory. Their meal at an exclusive restaurant had been a nightmare of awkwardness. "We didn't even make it through dinner."

"Was it that bad?"

"Yeah, it was." She could've enjoyed his monumental discomfort and considered it a sweet serve of karma, but she hadn't. He'd fumbled with the cutlery, guzzled the wine, and hadn't taken a bite of any of the extremely expensive meals. "He's not the dating type."

Shay slid the tequila sunrise across the bar but continued to grip the glass. "I gather things ended amicably if he reinstated your membership." She continued holding the alcohol hostage. "But if you being here is some form of retribution, I'm going to have to ask you to leave. I don't want any drama on his first night back."

"Drama? I'm not here to—"

"I like you." Shay lowered her voice, shooting a conspiratorial look over Pamela's shoulder as she released the glass. "Please don't make me kick you out."

"Kick who out?" Bryan's delicious, deep growl tickled her neck, the sound having the ability to burst ovaries in a ten-mile radius. "What did I miss?"

He swiveled her stool, dragging her attention to his ruggedly perfect face. His beard had been cropped, the blond strands shorter, revealing more of the man he hid beneath. She'd never get sick of staring at him, not when he looked at her with affection and ownership. Tonight, there was something else, too.

Was he nervous?

"Apparently, our break-up." She feigned a glare. "You told your friends we weren't dating anymore?"

His lush lips curved, setting off a chain reaction to

transform his features into something entirely stunning, and maybe even a little sweet. "We're not."

"True." She leaned in, swiping her mouth leisurely across his. His responding growl carried into her belly, tickling all the way down to her pussy. "But I think you've given them the wrong impression."

"You're still together?" Shay shrieked, stealing the attention of the room.

Numerous people stopped what they were doing—the drinking, the kissing, the fucking—and turned to face them.

"Subtle," Bryan grated. "Real fucking subtle, Shay."

Pamela wove a hand around his neck and kept him close. She loved this man. Not that he knew it. The L-word was extremely significant to him. Without the love of his parents, he considered the emotion to be the holy grail of humanity. She didn't expect to ever hear the declaration from his lips. But she took solace in telling herself his adoration and commitment were signs of something parallel.

"Why did you give your friends the wrong impression?" she whispered.

He'd changed during their time together. Each day, he opened up a little more, sharing tidbits about his past, giving enough to satisfy her concern. Apparently, that translucent behavior ended when he came to work.

"I had to keep you to myself for as long as possible." He leaned back to stare at her. "I didn't want to keep fielding questions about us every time I took a breath. I needed it to be you and me for a while."

"What the hell is going on?" Shay slapped her hands against the bar.

"See?" he drawled. "She's a hemorrhoid we'll never get rid of."

"I am not," the bartender snapped. "You're too secretive. Maybe if you shared every once in a while."

Bryan shook his head, his nose brushing Pamela's. "I don't want to share."

"You're lucky you're cute." She nibbled his lower lip. "But it's time to tell her. Don't be mean."

His chest rumbled, the predatory sound tickling her nipples as he slid his hands around her hips and cupped her ass. "We're not dating, Shay," he muttered between kisses. "We're living together."

Pamela smiled and sank into his affection while the bartender flung questions their way, over and over, one after another, until her voice approached a yell and Leo, T.J., and Cassie joined the inquisition. Not once did Bryan allow their kiss to break. He kept their bodies fused—lips and hips— while his tongue teased hers with gentle swirls.

She couldn't get enough of him or his arrogant demands. Not now, and definitely not when he'd dragged her from their first date and announced they needed to skip the irritating formalities and move in together.

Bryan hadn't functioned well under his preconceived notions of what a romantic relationship should be. He'd needed to create his own rules. And the unscheduled fast-forward into a cemented commitment had worked for them both.

She loved the stability and devotion. He enjoyed keeping her on her toes.

Not once had they looked back.

He wasn't anything like she'd anticipated. She'd already known they'd set sheets aflame in the bedroom. But away from the sex and the seduction, he was the most attentive and protective man she'd ever met.

Selfless, too.

Tonight, he surprised her all over again with his gentle devotion. In a sex club, for the first time as a couple, she'd thought he would've been in predator mode—all hands, teeth, and gyrating body parts.

This smooth tenderness was a million times better.

He inched back, those blue eyes slaying her with their passion. "Are you ready for the inquisition?"

She nodded, taking the seconds of their locked gaze to try to read him. When he swung toward his friends, she remained clueless.

T.J. and Cassie huddled beside them near the stools. Shay and Leo stood behind the bar.

Shay cocked a hip, a manicured brow rising. "You've got some ex—"

Leo clapped a hand over his girlfriend's mouth, softening the restriction with a kiss to her forehead.

"Are you happy?" Cassie asked over the growing enthusiasm in the room.

"That's your first question?" Bryan scoffed. "Great. This is going to take all night."

"That's our only question," Leo clarified. "You don't like to share, and we don't need to pry. We just want to make sure you're happy." He dropped his hand from Shay's face and poured himself a glass of bourbon. "Isn't that right, Shay?"

She grunted. "Speak for yourself. I want all the gory details."

"There are no gory details." Bryan wrapped a hand around Pamela's waist, squeezing tight. "Dating didn't work, so we moved in together."

"But you're happy?" T.J. asked.

"Yes." His response was simple. No inflection. No emotion. No bullshit. "Are we done now?"

Pamela hid her disappointment. She didn't want him to gush and brag about their relationship. She just wanted... Something. Anything to match the man he became in the privacy of his own home. Here in the bar, he'd regressed to

225

being the closed off, tight-lipped guy she first met. Even his posture seemed stiff.

Leo inclined his head, raised his glass in salute, and then walked for the end of the bar.

Discussion over.

"Yep. That's all." Cassie beamed. "I'm so pleased for you both." She clapped Bryan on the shoulder and strode away, dragging her husband along with her.

Shay did a repeat of her eye-roll, not saying a word as she side-stepped and requested a drink order from a waiting patron with a jerk of her chin.

That was it. The inquisition had finished before it had begun.

"You hid our relationship because of that?" she asked.

"That's not normal," he muttered. "I think they're lulling us into a false sense of security."

"Is that why you're anxious?"

He stiffened, not meeting her gaze.

She'd nailed it. He *was* anxious. "What is it? I thought you were excited about tonight."

They'd discussed the complexity of returning to the Vault. It was their first major test. The trust and responsibility of being committed while participating in a sex club wasn't something to disregard without a second, third, or fourth thought.

He frowned. "I don't know what you're talking about."

Now he was lying? "Bryan? What's going on?"

"*Shit*," he muttered under his breath. "Look, I have something planned. I'm just not sure how it will turn out."

Her stomach flipped. What plans could put this experienced man on edge? "You're never nervous when it comes to sex."

"Exactly." He cleared his throat and stood tall. "*Hey*." He raised his voice, cutting through the moans and whimpers. "I need everyone's attention."

Her heart fluttered as the room fell under his command. Couples stopped fucking. People stepped out of the adjoining rooms to hear what he had to say. Even Cassie and T.J. looked on in confusion from the far corner.

"As you all know, this is my first night back—"

Wolf whistles and cheers sliced through the air.

"Come on, guys." He hushed the excitement with raised hands. "As I was saying, I haven't been down here since before I canceled the demonstration night. Unfortunately, the original plan didn't work out, but tonight I'd like to give you all a taste of what's in store when I reorganize the class."

He faced her and held out a hand.

"Bryan?" She glanced around the room, unsure what was going on. "What are you doing?"

"I need you to help assist me in a tiny preview."

She shook her head. *No.* No, no, no. She'd barely been prepared for what could've happened in the dark shadows on their own, let alone under a microscope.

Everyone stared at them, the simmering excitement in the air tickling her skin.

"I don't think I'm ready for this."

His anxiety faded under the brilliance of his smirk. "You will be." The promise was wicked. Confident. Entirely undeniable.

She reached for her drink and gulped some of the liquid.

"Don't drink too much." His heat closed in to envelop her, his lips finding her neck. "You don't want to be numb for this."

Yes, she did.

If it weren't for his anxiety, she would've indulged in the upcoming naughtiness with bounding delight. Her nipples already tingled. Her panties had turned into a Slip 'N Slide.

She loved every opportunity to be an exhibitionist in the safe environment of the Vault.

But Bryan was worried about something. The fear pulsed off him in waves.

"We should talk about this first." The weight of the room's interest bore down on her.

"Trust me."

"This has nothing to do with trust. I've never seen you anything other than one hundred percent confident when it comes to sex. Whatever you're concerned about is starting to concern me."

"Come on," a man called from the back of the room. "Bring on the demo."

Bryan slid a hand into her loose hair and cupped the back of her head. "I was worried about dumping this on you. That's all. I didn't want you to anticipate what was coming, and not telling you made me feel like a guilty little bitch."

She studied him, unsure what to believe. "Are you bullshitting me?"

"When have I ever done that?" He smirked, making it ten times harder for her to trust her intuition.

"Are you sure everything is okay between us?" That was all that mattered. She didn't care about anything else.

"We're exactly where I want us to be at this point in time." He entwined their hands and tugged her from the stool. He led her through the mingling crowd, weaving through the condensing throng without effort. "The sooner we get this over with, the sooner I get you all to myself."

Leo and T.J. quickly rearranged furniture, creating space. Ottomans were shoved toward the wall. Sofas were turned and swiveled. Everything was strategically placed to face the large bed in the center of the room, the cream satin sheets gleaming under the overhead lights.

Bryan stopped at the side of the mattress and kissed her

knuckles. "You're not going to fuck this up. However this turns out, it's because of me, okay?"

She nodded.

"Okay?" he growled, his drawn brows demanding a vocal response.

"Okay, you big brute."

With a subtle glide, his expression transformed from tight concern to gentle appreciation. Maybe even pride. "And don't you forget it."

"I already have." She knew him better now, better than anyone who believed this man was harsh and heartless. Past his sterile exterior, he was the exact opposite.

"All right, everyone." He scoped the audience of half-dressed patrons. "This is only going to be a taste of what's to come. On the actual demonstration night, I plan to discuss a range of different techniques. We'll go over the benefits of edging, and how consistency or surprise can affect women in different ways. But tonight, it's all about reading signs."

He crooked a finger at her, encouraging her onto the bed. "Lie down close to me. You need to stay in reach."

She stood immobile, her heart galloping into her throat. This would bring her exhibitionism to a whole new level—from amateur to professor.

"Don't worry." He held out a hand. "I promise to look after you." His grin was sly and cocky, the opposite of reassuring.

He didn't make sense. One moment he seemed restless and skittish. The next he exuded his ingrained confident sexuality without flaw.

"You're going to have a lot of explaining to do later. You know that, right?"

He inclined his head. "I know, sweetheart."

She slid her palm into his and allowed him to help her onto the raised bed. He guided her to lie close to the side of the mattress, the tiny overhead lights beaming down, bathing her in a glow before the shadowed audience.

"Gorgeous." Appreciation ebbed off him. "I think you're going to have more than a few admirers after this."

Her cheeks heated, from his words and the crowd's whispers of affirmation.

"Your blush does things to me, sweetheart."

"Me, too," another man muttered.

She chuckled and shook her head. "Just get started, would you?"

"You all heard the lady. We need to get this show on the road." He pivoted to the crowd of thirty-odd people, all of them silent with expectation. "Your job tonight is to study this flawless woman. I want you to be able to pinpoint those barely recognizable signs to learn just how subtle a partner can be during sex."

Their scrutiny bore down on her, tickling her skin and heightening her awareness. She breathed in their interest, letting it coat her in tingling carnality. But something else made the pressure between her thighs intensify. Something she'd grown to crave each day from this addictive man.

"See that?" His short, sharp glance captured everything. "Her breathing has increased, and I haven't even touched her yet. Can anyone tell me why she's already aroused?"

"Alcohol?" someone asked.

"Nope," Shay called. "She didn't even finish her first drink."

"She's in a sex club. Of course she's aroused," a man drawled.

"Wrong." Bryan verbally slapped away the comment. "She isn't new to the scene. It's not like watching you fool around is going to send her into a panting mess. Try again."

"The anticipation?" a feminine voice asked.

"Maybe, but I wouldn't bet my house on it." He held

Pamela's gaze, deciphering every move she made. Every breath. Every thought. "Anyone else have a suggestion?"

Silence followed, not a whisper of an answer coming forward.

His focus held her in a trance, her breaths becoming gasps.

"Your eyes," she admitted. "Your confidence."

"I hoped you'd say that." He gifted her with a subtle grin. "Most women are attracted to knowledge. Problem is, every woman is different, which means nobody can become complacent. There's always a learning curve with a new partner, no matter how good you think you are. The trick to becoming an expert is to read who you're with. Never stop searching for signals."

He took a step toward the end of the bed, aligning himself with her feet. "You have to acknowledge what isn't being said, because your partner may lie for numerous reasons. Maybe they lack confidence. Or don't trust you enough. Maybe they're shy. Or don't want to hurt your feelings."

His hand reached out, the approach a slow, tormenting tease. She could feel his touch before the lone fingertip grazed her ankle, the slight brush scorching in its wake.

"Nothing is more rewarding than a sexually satisfied woman." He spoke softly, the trail of fire ascending along her calf. "Take your time exploring their body. Make her think it's a game, when all along, you're creeping further and further under her skin. Learning her secrets."

She tried not to move, not to flinch. Staying quiet became difficult. The further that lone fingertip trailed, the more her body reacted without her permission, jolting and glitching like a Richter scale in an apocalyptic earthquake.

"How do y'all think I'm doing so far?"

"Her breathing is still getting faster," Cassie offered.

"Yes. But what else?" His caress crept higher, over her

knee, along the inside of her thigh. "Has anyone noticed her muscle spasms? They're flowing along her leg, preceding my touch, anticipating my next move."

"She's tilted in your direction, too," T.J. added. "Not much, but a little."

"Those are the tiny signs you need to look for. Anything deliberate could be a lie, for the reasons I've mentioned. These almost imperceptible changes are the things that mean the most. Especially those beautiful eyes dilating."

She was ready to ditch the imperceptible signs and drag him to the bed by his hair. How could a lone finger torment her like this?

No. It wasn't the solitary stroke. She couldn't forget that. It was his stare. His voice. His infallible expertise. The list increased with every blink.

His aftershave. His dress sense. His erotic selflessness.

There wasn't one thing about this man that didn't turn her on.

Not one thing that didn't encourage her to want to grind her thighs together.

She cleared the gravel from her throat and swallowed to soothe the burn.

He paused in his moment of sexual prowess, giving way to sweet sincerity. "How are you doing?"

"Fine, thanks." Her betraying voice broke.

People chuckled, some snorted, while Bryan grinned down at her, his admiration a living, breathing thing.

The fire reignited at mid-thigh, sliding to her garter.

She licked her lips, overheating, hyperventilating.

Everyone watched them, their fascination rushing through her. There was no condemnation from the group, only awe and enjoyment. Every single person had pinpoint focus on her gratification.

He slid a finger under her garter and pulled tight to release it with a snap.

"Ouch," she hissed.

"Now, that right there is a blindingly brilliant display of something I've done wrong. And I'm not talking about the verbal cue. Yes, she also flinched, which is another obvious sign, but if she was shy and tried to suppress her reactions, we'd still be able to rely on the rigidity of her posture and the way she tilted her legs away."

"She pulled back into the mattress, too," a woman offered.

"Exactly." Bryan slid his finger along her garter, soothing the sting beneath. "Even if she did gasp or whimper or moan, her body is pulling away. This is when you check your ego at the door and acknowledge your partner didn't enjoy what you dished out."

Pamela froze, not realizing the signals she was sending. Her cheeks tingled. Her chest and belly, too.

"Now," he continued, "once you fuck up, you need to make amends. Mistakes are common. All you need to do is work them to your advantage."

He added another finger to the soothing slide along her garter. Gradually, those searching digits skimmed higher and higher, gliding inward to the sensitive spot where her inner thigh met the crotch of her panties. She jolted, overwrought with twirling knots inside her pussy.

"All better?" he teased.

"You're a horrible man." She glared, earning herself another laugh from the crowd.

His touch delved under the elastic and hovered in place, not advancing to his prize. Back and forth he rubbed right beneath her panty line, turning the erogenous zone into an orgasm trigger set to detonate. He was going to make her come without penetration.

Again.

"I want to keep hearing observations. Call them out. Tell me what you see, because from my point of view, she's a kaleidoscope of signals."

She whimpered and sank her teeth into her lower lip.

He was there. *Right* there. Less than an inch from her pulsing pussy. Yet, he seemed a mile away. The confidence in his focus told her the height of her bliss would come when he allowed it.

"Her back arched," a man called.

"She thrust her breasts."

"Her eyes rolled."

Breathing became difficult as overlapping observations filled the room.

"She's panting."

"Clutching the sheet."

"She keeps swallowing."

Bryan encroached, those fingertips nudging closer and closer until finally he slid through her arousal, the smooth glide exquisite. Almost perfection. Just not quite enough.

She needed a little more. The slightest penetration. A swipe across her clit.

"Her hips are lifted toward you."

"She's shaking."

"She closed her eyes."

Oh, God.

He stopped. The heavenly glide ceased. Those wonderful fingers escaped her panties.

She blinked up at him, collapsing into the mattress as frustrated tears blurred her vision. This was torture. Pure, hysteria-rich suffering.

"Not yet, sweetheart." His own suffering bled through his words. "There's one more thing I want to do before I have you all to myself."

"Please, Bryan." She clenched her thighs together. "This is killing me."

"I know."

He reached out a hand and she grasped his offering, allowing him to guide her into a seated position.

"I'm giving you all one last chance to analyze her." He sat on the edge of the mattress and patted his thighs. "Come here."

She frowned, frantically trying to figure out what came next.

"It's okay. This won't take long." He grabbed her wrist and led her to sit on his lap, facing the crowd.

Her limbs trembled with need. A sheen of sweat coated her skin. It took all her self-control not to turn and bury her face in his neck. One more whispered plea and she knew he'd give her what she needed. He'd end both their torment.

He parted her thighs with his hands, encouraging her legs to drape over his, exposing the soaked crotch of her panties.

She vibrated, thrummed. She'd been infused with hyper-sensitivity. Even the subtle scratch of his suit material made her whimper.

"I want you to watch her closely." His voice became low, brutal in its command. "I need you to focus and make sure you read all those signs."

Her breath hitched, the anticipation killing her. Her heart threatened to explode, the pulsing muscles on fire behind her ribcage.

"Are you ready, sweetheart?"

She nodded as he guided her loose hair away from her shoulder to place his lips at her ear.

"This time the test comes in words," he whispered. "Let's see what reactions I can inspire."

She nodded, ready and oh, so willing to hear his dirty talk.

"You sure you're ready?"

"Yes," she gasped. She was ready for this to be over so she could jump him, smash her lips to his, and drag his body beneath hers.

"Okay."

She heard his swallow and felt the tease of his beard against her cheek.

"Ella..." His voice was barely audible, leaving everyone clueless to their conversation. "I've been wanting to tell you this for a while. But I didn't know how you'd react."

She nodded, the frantic bob of her head trying to encourage a speedier outcome.

"Ella..." He stopped, sighed, those hands on her thighs becoming sweaty. "I love you."

Arousal vanished. Noise, too.

There was nothing.

No thoughts. No comprehension. Only a slow repeat of his gentle declaration through her mind.

"That doesn't look good." Distant words fractured her daze.

"Whatever you said wiped away the lust."

"You blew it, Brute. She's not horny anymore."

Those three words had been a dream she never thought she'd experience. They were too important to him. Too special. Three words fractured her, making everything unstable—her heart, her mind, her emotions.

Strong hands gripped her waist, lifting her, turning her limp body to sit sideways on his lap.

"Ella?" His blue eyes blinked through apprehension, his vulnerability unmasked for everyone to see. "I should've kept my mouth shut, shouldn't I?"

"No." She shook her head. Her tongue tangled with all the things she needed to say. All the things he needed to hear. "Not at all."

"What happened?" a woman yelled. "What's going on?"

His nostrils flared, the harshness returning to his features. "I should've done this somewhere else."

"Why didn't you?" The questioned tumbled from her mouth. "Why now? Why here?"

She didn't understand. It would've been so much easier for him to share this moment in private. Alone. Without a mass of scrutiny.

"I can read your body like it's my own, sweetheart. But when it comes to reading your emotions, I'm clueless. I needed their help to gauge your reaction." He released a caustic laugh. "I guess it didn't work in my favor."

"Of course it did. I'm just shocked. That's all."

"You're about to cry."

"No." She swiped at the lone tear that broke free. "I'm not."

He raised a brow, silently calling bullshit.

"Well, I am, but it's because I'm happy. I never thought I'd hear those words from you."

He stiffened. "Because I'm a heartless asshole?"

"Bryan, I know that declaration means the world to you. And I..."

"You didn't realize you mean more than the world to me?"

Her chest heated, warmth and relief flooding her in equal doses. "I wasn't sure."

"Be sure, Ella," he whispered. "There's nothing more important to me than you. No matter how you feel in return."

His fingers glided along her jaw, holding her in place as he leaned in for a chaste kiss. The brush of lips lasted a second before he pulled away.

No. She wanted more. Needed everything.

She stood, changing her position to straddle his lap.

"That poor excuse for a kiss isn't going to satisfy." She poked him in the chest, earning a snicker. "Not after you've teased me to mindlessness."

"Welcome to my life. That's what it's like living with you every damn day."

She smiled and leaned her head against his shoulder, running her arms around his waist while his wove around her back.

His feelings mimicked her own. Her adoration and affection were reciprocated. The brutal man she'd once thought heartless was more tender and loving than anyone could imagine.

"Are we still supposed to be watching?" someone asked, the silence of growing confusion changing the once heated atmosphere.

Neither of them responded. They didn't move, didn't speak as they continued to pretend the world didn't exist.

For her, nothing existed.

Only him.

Only her.

"Bryan?" she whispered.

He placed a delicate butterfly kiss to her neck. "Yeah, sweetheart?"

"I love you more."

Every muscle beneath her tightened. His arms tensed around her back.

"Oh, shit," someone muttered from the crowd. "What the fuck is going on?"

"I'm confused. Is this part of the demonstration?" a woman asked.

"I don't think so." Leo's voice carried over the growing speculation. "That's it, folks. This is the end of the show. Let's give them some privacy, okay?"

Shuffling feet moved around the bed. Murmured words brushed her ears. But she didn't let him go. She didn't flinch in her unwavering hold as the room returned to its usual broadcast of dirty talk and indulgence.

"Nobody has said that to me before." His hold tightened, squeezing her like a lifeline. "I never knew what it would feel like."

"What does it feel like?"

"I don't know." He shook his head against hers. "I guess it feels like I'm not alone anymore."

"You're not. You never will be." She'd make him see. One day at a time. No matter how long it took. "Take me home, Bryan. I don't want to be here right now."

"Good decision." He kissed her forehead and stood, keeping her locked around his waist like a child. "But first, I want to hear those words again."

"What words?" She grinned, unsuccessfully playing dumb.

"You know what I'm talking about."

"I do. But I want you to ask properly."

His jaw tensed, but he faced the vulnerability head-on, tilting his chin as he stared her down. "Tell me you love me, Ella."

Pain exploded in her chest. The most delicious and fulfilling pain she'd ever felt. "I love you, Bryan Munro. I love every damn thing about you."

PLEASE CONSIDER LEAVING A REVIEW ON YOUR BOOK RETAILER WEBSITE OR GOODREADS

ALSO BY EDEN SUMMERS

RECKLESS BEAT SERIES

Blind Attraction (Reckless Beat #1)

Passionate Addiction (Reckless Beat #2)

Reckless Weekend (Reckless Beat #2.5)

Undesired Lust (Reckless Beat #3)

Sultry Groove (Reckless Beat #4)

Reckless Rendezvous (Reckless Beat #4.5)

Undeniable Temptation (Reckless Beat #5)

THE VAULT SERIES

A Shot of Sin (The Vault #1)

Union of Sin (The Vault #2)

Brutal Sin (The Vault #3)

More titles can be found at:

www.edensummers.com

ABOUT THE AUTHOR

Eden Summers is a true blue Aussie, living in regional New South Wales with her two energetic young boys and a quick witted husband.

In late 2010, Eden's romance obsession could no longer be sated by reading alone, so she decided to give voice to the sexy men and sassy women in her mind.

Eden can't resist alpha dominance, dark features and sarcasm in her fictional heroes and loves a strong heroine who knows when to bite her tongue but also serves retribution with a feminine smile on her face.

If you'd like access to exclusive information and giveaways, join Eden Summers' newsletter.

For more information:

www.edensummers.com

eden@edensummers.com